DEBT OF HONOUR

Trouble explodes when English blue-blood Lord Ewen brings sheep to Jameson County. Sergeant Brad Saunders arrives to find Lord Ewen's sheep being systematically slaughtered by a masked gang. The likeliest suspect is Morgan Holliger as his Lazy Y outfit is facing bankruptcy. But nothing is quite what it seems and finally Brad is forced to take sides. He faces danger every step of the way as he fights to restore law and order.

D. A. HORNCASTLE

DEBT OF HONOUR

Complete and Unabridged

LINFORD
Leicester

First published in Great Britain in 1996 by
Robert Hale Limited
London

First Linford Edition
published 1998
by arrangement with
Robert Hale Limited
London

British Library CIP Data

Horncastle, D. A.
    Debt of honour.—Large print ed.—
Linford western library
    1. Western stories
    2. Large type books
    I. Title
    823.9'14 [F]

    ISBN 0–7089–5202–X   ᴜʰᴜ 31.3.98

Published by
F. A. Thorpe (Publishing) Ltd.
Anstey, Leicestershire

Set by Words & Graphics Ltd.
Anstey, Leicestershire
Printed and bound in Great Britain by
T. J. International Ltd., Padstow, Cornwall

This book is printed on acid-free paper

FOR JULIE

1

THE cattle trail crawling north-west from San Antonio over the Balcones Escarpment onto the Edwards Plateau was a lonely one, but the tall, well-built man sitting atop the big bay stallion had no fears on that score, for most of his life was spent alone. Indeed, in this lawless land, a man was better off in his own company — provided he kept his wits about him and a weapon close at hand.

Here the terrain was changing almost imperceptibly from the stunted scrub and prickly pear thickets of the arid south-west to a more undulating countryside of rolling volcanic hills affording a prospect of sundry rocky outcrops standing like islands in a sea of grama grass out of which stands of scrubby live oak appeared like ships' masts on a storm-tossed sea. This was

1

the Texas hill country, a seeming forsaken land, until you realized how well it concealed vast numbers of cattle grazing in scattered groups, their presence revealed only by the crackle of a dry twig in the undergrowth or the glimpse of the statuesque silhouette of a longhorn on the skyline.

The crudely drawn map which Sergeant Brad Saunders had folded neatly and slotted into his vest pocket told him he was still some 30 miles short of Chanceville.

Now Brad did not know Chanceville, for it lay on the outer limit of the Texas Rangers Special Company's remit, but from what Lieutenant Hall had told him, once he arrived, he was going to be a very busy man . . .

"I've had a request, more like a plea I guess, for help from the sheriff of Jameson County," Hall told Brad. "Not only does he have problems controlling the town but he reckons there's a whole heap of trouble brewing between the cattlemen and sheepherders."

"Then that means trouble aplenty," Brad replied with a grimace.

Hall nodded.

"Jameson County," Brad mused. "Ain't Tex Grant the sheriff there?"

Hall nodded. "You know him?"

"No, but the boys say he's OK."

"Which probably means he's doin' his best against all the odds," Hall said dryly. "If that's the case, I guess he wouldn't ask for help if he doesn't need it. Very well, Sergeant Saunders, I can't really spare you, but I guess you'd best go to Chanceville and lend Grant a hand. It shouldn't take long."

Brad had left Lieutenant Hall's office in San Antonio two days ago. Since breaking camp at dawn he'd been riding loose in the saddle, alone with his thoughts, but at one with his environment, always passively aware of what was happening around him. The buzzards he spotted circling about a mile off the trail were not an unusual sight and he might not have bothered, but the report of a distant gunshot aroused his curiosity.

He reined in Blaze, dismounted and taking out his brass-bound spy-glass, focused it on the spot where the birds were circling. A slight movement caught his attention and then suddenly a group of riders burst into view out of the low scrub. Brad counted five as they headed at a fast lick away from him towards some low hills, a cloud of dust screening their retreat. He snapped the instrument shut and pondered. Five men riding off hell-for-leather after a single gunshot? He'd best take a look . . .

He remounted and the big stallion responded instantly to a hint from his spurs. A few hundred yards off the trail, they startled a handful of grazing sheep hiding in a mesquite thicket.

Brad reined in and stared at the bolting animals. To a man born and raised in the Panhandle, the spectacle was both unfamiliar and disturbing. It spelt trouble.

He was drawing closer to his goal now and, as a precaution, he drew his Peacemaker, reining Blaze in to a slow walk, edging the stallion forward, straining to see what lay immediately ahead.

The stallion snorted and pricked up his ears, at the sudden flutter of wings. Brad crashed him through a gap in a thicket and emerged on to a short stretch of open grassland.

Ahead lay a post and wire pen. As he moved nearer, Brad saw that although it appeared full of sheep, it seemed strangely silent. Puzzled at the lack of movement, he edged in closer, seeking the reason for it.

He was totally unprepared for what he saw. Hardened as he was to the harrowing sights of a battlefield, he gagged when he saw the corpses. The slaughter was complete. Not a single animal was left alive. A foul odour was already permeating the fresh morning air. The buzzards were so gorged they could barely disentangle their claws free from their prey's blood-stained fleeces and their wings struggled to lift them clear of the ground as they flopped ponderously around hissing like angry snakes before lumbering into flight at his approach.

The carcasses were still warm, confirming that the massacre had happened recently. The unfortunate animals had been despatched mostly by having their throats slit, but some had been bludgeoned to death in the cruellest of fashions. He estimated that around a couple of hundred had been killed — a task which must have kept five men occupied for some considerable time. A broken fence post revealed the place from where the handful of sheep he had seen earlier must have broken free. The only living thing was a burro, shivering on the end of its tether to a broken fence post.

Brad cut the animal loose and knee-haltered it before carrying out a thorough inspection of the ground surrounding the pen. From the mish-mash of hoof and boot marks he confirmed that five riders had been in the vicinity of the pen. But there had also been one other . . .

Suddenly, he bethought himself — *where was the herder?*

Continuing his search, he soon discovered the corpse of a dog. It had been shot. Underneath it he found a carbine. A cursory inspection revealed it to be a twin-triggered Franklin Wesson with an octagonal barrel — a sporting gun — not the kind of weapon carried by an outlaw, but just the type that would be used by a peace loving man tending sheep and needing to shoot for the pot.

Further search revealed a blanket and knapsack in the corner of the corral. Inside the knapsack he found a copy of the Bible in a Spanish translation. It was well thumbed, but there was no name on the fly-leaf. Brad gathered the man's meagre belongings together before resuming his patient search for sign. Within a few minutes he found a spot where the grass was flecked with blood.

He straightened up, puzzled. Blaze and the burro tugged speculatively at the closely shorn grass nearby as Brad went down on his haunches, his keen eyes scanning the grass. From the lie of the strands it was clear that the man had crawled away and Brad followed the trail of flattened grass and bloodstains into a thicket until he found him.

At first Brad thought he was dead, but as he bent down over the prostrate figure, he detected a slight movement. *He was still alive!*

Closer inspection revealed he had been shot through the chest. From the bubble of blood on his lips, Brad figured the bullet must have touched the lung. Puzzled at first, Brad stared with mounting anger at the man's ravaged back until it dawned on him that he must have been flogged before he had been shot.

Brad bent down and picked up the slight body in one easy movement and returned to the spot where he had tethered Blaze.

As he laid the man face down Brad bent low to listen as he figured he was trying to say something, but the herder was too weak to speak. Brad opened his water bottle and with a little patience he managed to make him take a few drops. Then he went over to Blaze, opened his saddle-bag, took out a field dressing and used it to staunch the trickle of blood from the bullet wound. Finally, he took his own spare shirt and laid it gently over the man's back before setting himself the task of making a crude travois from some thin saplings he cut with his Bowie knife.

The sun rose hot and as he worked Brad was aware of the buzzards perched in the low trees, watching him with suspicious eyes, preening their blood-encrusted feathers, not daring to return to their grisly feast until he hitched the travois to Blaze and, leading the burro, walked his cavalcade back to the Chanceville trail.

Of necessity, progress was slow and Brad made a couple of stops, once to brew java for himself and each time administer a few drops of water to the injured man. Despite every effort, Brad couldn't even get him to speak his name. By noon the sun was blazing hot and he became concerned that the herder might not survive for his pulse was growing weaker. The man clearly needed rest and proper medical attention.

Brad had almost given up hope, when to his relief, he spotted a coil of smoke rising on the horizon. Viewed through his spy-glass, it rose from what appeared to be a substantial dwelling, probably a cattleman's ranch house. As he rode on he passed by groups of grazing steers. Their flanks were branded with crosses, a brand which Brad had never seen used before.

A few minutes later, a neatly painted

sign announced that a turning off the trail led to:

THE IRON CROSS RANCH
PROP. BARON von FAULKENBURG

Clearly, the herder's only chance of survival was to rest up at this ranch while he rode on for medical help. Without hesitating, Brad left the trail to Chanceville and followed it.

He had not been riding for long before it was apparent that he was being followed. The rider made no attempt at concealment and drew closer; it was clear he was keeping Brad under surveillance.

After a mile or so, Brad grew tired of this cat-and-mouse game. He waited until the trail passed through a spinney of live oak. As soon as he was out of sight, he stopped and did not have long to wait before a young cowboy appeared.

"You lookin' fer someone, boy?" Brad enquired.

"That's the question we're askin', mister," a harsh voice said from behind.

Brad whirled round, his hand snaking for the Peacemaker holstered to his right hip.

"I wouldn't try any of that."

Brad's hand froze in mid-air.

The man who had surprised him was much older than his youthful decoy. He was dressed in the typical gear of the range cowboy — a faded striped collarless shirt, a red bandana spotted white, calf-skin vest and levis — and he looked completely at home with the Colt he was pointing at Brad.

"Where d'you think you're goin', mister?"

Brad was taken aback at the man's peremptory tone.

"Well now, I got a badly injured man here," Brad replied. "I guess I thought I'd stop by at this ranch and get me some help."

The man eyed the man lying on the travois curiously.

"It's the 'breed," his companion said, making no attempt to conceal the contempt in his voice.

"D'you know him?" Brad asked sharply.

"I've seen him around. He's one of Ewen's mutton punchers. But I can't put no name to him. Best take him into town. There's a doctor there."

"And how far might that be?" Brad enquired.

"About two hours' ride," came the reply.

Brad felt his hackles rising. All-out opposition he could handle, but casual indifference irritated him beyond endurance.

"You mean flat out on a fast hoss?"

His sarcasm wasn't lost on his audience.

"Now see here," Brad continued without waiting for a reply. "This guy's had a floggin' to within nigh an inch of his life and he's also been shot. It seems to me he ain't gonna make the journey into Chanceville. Now I figure

13

to leave him here in your care while I ride in and ask the doc to call in the morning."

"You heard what I just said, mister. Get that mutton-punching 'breed outa here."

Brad spread his hands wide in a gesture of helplessness. "Maybe iffen I could speak with Baron von Faulkenburg . . ."

"I am the baron's top-screw," the man snapped. "And I'm tellin' you, mister, injured or not, mutton-punchers ain't welcome round here. So turn around and get movin'."

The snort of a horse attracted the men's attention. Brad's eyes widened in surprise when he saw it was a woman approaching them. She was wearing a long-sleeved blouse and divided riding skirt. A stetson, held by its leather *barboquejo*, rested lightly on her shoulders, revealing black hair drawn back to leave a parting down the centre. High-moulded cheekbones gave her face an appearance which

14

was austerely handsome rather than beautiful. Wearing a leather divided riding skirt, she was sitting astride a magnificent white Andalucian stallion.

"What is going on here, Mr Pate?" she demanded.

Her English was good, but Brad had met enough immigrants in Texas to realize that the woman's accent was German in origin. As she drew closer, Brad figured that she was in her late twenties.

"Ain't no need for you to concern yourself with this business, ma'am," the top-screw said. "I'm just seein' off a couple drifters."

Brad watched in admiration as the woman manoeuvred her horse expertly in order to look at the stretcher.

"Drifters, you say?"

"Yep."

The woman's eyes narrowed as she looked at the herder. "Who is this man? What has happened to him? Why have you brought him here?"

Brad took a deep breath and resisted

the temptation to show his irritation at her rat-a-tat of questions. For answer he dismounted and drew back the shirt he'd laid across the sheepherder's back. She gasped as it revealed the mass of red-raw contusions.

"Don't know his name," Brad said. "I found him out on the range 'bout ten miles back along with a whole heap of dead sheep."

The woman took a deep breath, plainly taken aback.

"Mr Pate, have this man taken up to the house immediately."

"But . . . "

"Do it!"

Brad watched Pate closely as the woman spoke, but there was no mistaking the decisive Teutonic hauteur in her command. If the foreman was resentful at being given orders by the woman, he showed no sign of it.

"As you wish, ma'am," he deferred.

There was a flurry of hooves as the woman rode off. After issuing a curt instruction to his cowhand, Pate did likewise, but in the opposite direction.

Escorted by the cowhand, who made it clear he wasn't interested in further discussion, Brad rode the final mile with the travois and burro in tow until they arrived at the ranch house.

The house was well-built from timber and adobe, clearly the home of a very wealthy family. The cowhand led Brad past the barn and through the dog trot between the cookhouse and bunkhouse to a stone-flagged courtyard at the back of the house.

"Wait here," he ordered. "I'll go fetch Liza."

He left Brad there and went into the servants' quarters. The place was so quiet, the only sound was the sough of the breeze through the blades accompanied by the rhythmic creaking from the gears in the windmill.

A few moments later a plump, black servant came bustling out of the house. She was wearing an apron and both her pudgy forearms were caked to the elbows with flour. The whites of her eyes rolled skywards and she clucked like an old hen when she saw the sheepherder's wound and lacerated back.

"Now you just bring him right inside," she told Brad.

The cowhand made no attempt to assist. Brad laid the injured man face down on a blanket the woman had already draped across the kitchen table. Satisfied he was in safe hands, Brad went back into the courtyard. The cowhand had gone.

There was nothing to keep him here, Brad decided. Best ride into town and ask the doctor to call and then meet with the sheriff.

He had one foot in the stirrup when there was a clattering of hooves and the woman he had met out on the range cantered into the courtyard.

"Do not go. I wish to speak further with you."

When a woman like this spoke like that, there was no arguing . . .

2

"EXCUSE me, but I did not hear your name, Mr . . . ?"

Brad removed his hat. "Name's Saunders, ma'am, Sergeant Brad Saunders, Texas Rangers."

Her eyes widened. "You are a Texas Ranger? Why, I thought Mr Pate said you were a drifter!" she exclaimed.

"I guess he never asked," Brad said.

If she was aware of the irony in his voice, the woman gave no sign of it.

"My name is Augusta von Faulkenburg. I am the baron's daughter." She announced, rather than introduced herself.

There was no wedding ring on the hand she used to pat Blaze on the neck. Brad pondered the reason why she wasn't married. Eligible women were so rare they tended to be snapped up as soon as they appeared on the frontier.

"You have a very fine horse there, Sergeant Saunders. Why, he is almost as good as my Wotan."

Brad resisted the temptation to smile for he could see she was deadly serious.

"Ma'am, I'll stake my Blaze against any hoss over five miles," he drawled, rising to her bait. "But, right now, I guess I'd better be movin' out." He eased his horse forward. "With your permission, it's my intention to ride into Chanceville and ask the doctor to call here tomorrow."

"Very well," Augusta replied, with an imperious wave of her hand. "But before you leave, will you take tea with me?"

"That's very kind of you, ma'am, but please give your father my apologies, I'd best be on my way."

A spark of anger flashed in the woman's eyes. She was used to giving orders and clearly would not countenance a refusal.

"There is no need for you to hurry, Sergeant Saunders. My father is very ill otherwise I would introduce you to him but unfortunately he isn't well enough to receive visitors."

"I'm sorry to hear that, ma'am."

"As far as that injured man is concerned, you need not worry. I am expecting the doctor to call tomorrow. He will be able to attend the sheepherder while he is here."

"Thank you for your consideration, ma'am."

"So now you are in no hurry, you have time to take tea with me. You will forgive me if I do not change?"

Brad suppressed a smile as he nodded. This was living in the grand manner. If Augusta von Faulkenburg was as domineering as this, it was small wonder men had fought shy of her.

"My father has a great respect for the law," she continued. "He would never forgive me if I did not have an explanation of how a badly beaten man came to be left here by a Texas Ranger."

"Very well, ma'am."

She clapped her hands and a young Mexican groom appeared.

"Manuel — the horses. And mind that Sergeant Saunders will be leaving in one hour from now, so please attend to his first."

In spite of her overbearing demeanour Brad felt his respect rising for Augusta von Faulkenburg. Riding whip in one hand, tall and leggy in her Spanish leather riding boots, she strode ahead of him the length of a long stone-flagged corridor and opened a heavy oak door into a room comfortably furnished with an oak table and armchairs. Hunting trophies adorned the walls, wood carvings stood on the tables. There were covered chairs, oriental rugs — and wallpaper too, but then what else did he expect in the house of a wealthy German immigrant?

They sat several feet apart in chairs made from longhorn on either side of an enormous stone fireplace over the mantelpiece of which hung a massive oil painting of a man in military uniform.

He was standing in a forthright pose, holding his Prussian helmet under his arm. A woman, looking equally imperious, was sitting proudly in front of him, her hands folded in her lap.

"The Baron with my mother," Augusta said, indicating the portrait with the tip of her whip. "Papa was a general in the Prussian Army before he retired after the war with France. My mother died shortly before we emigrated to America."

For a fleeting moment, Brad saw the baron's haughty expression reflected in his daughter's face before allowing his eyes to wander further along the mantelpiece until they came to rest on two oval-framed photographs of much younger men, also in military uniform.

Augusta put down her riding whip and picked up one of the photographs.

"This is my eldest brother, Heinrich," she said, pointing to the medal on his chest. "He won the Iron Cross at Sedan. He was killed at the Siege of Paris."

"So that's how the ranch came to be named, I guess?"

Augusta nodded. "The Iron Cross has its origins in the arms of the Teutonic Knights. It is Prussia's highest award for bravery. My father was so proud of Heinrich. When he was killed it was almost more than he could bear."

She replaced the photograph and picked up the remaining one. "And this is Count Krantz, the man I was going to marry. He served in the same regiment as my brother. He was the colonel and my brother his adjutant. They were both killed by the same shell."

Brad listened in a respectful silence. She was referring to a war about which he had to confess he knew very little. The War Between the States had taken away his own youth and Texas was still paying the price in lawlessness. Wars were still being fought all over the globe. Would there ever be peace?

Augusta turned to face Brad, trying

hard to conceal her emotion. "After the war, I left Prussia and came to America with my father to help him to start a new life. But now he has cancer and the doctor has said he has only a few days to live."

"I'm sorry to hear that, ma'am," Brad said quietly.

They paused while a maid laid a tray of tea on a side table.

"Pearl, how is the baron?" Augusta asked her.

"He is still asleep, ma'am," the woman replied.

"Then we shall not disturb him."

Brad didn't like tea, but he was thirsty so he drank it from the exquisitely patterned Dresden china stoically, promising himself a mug of coffee to get rid of the taste as soon as it was practicable.

"So, instead of being the wife of a Prussian count touring the salons of Europe, I am now living in America and helping to run a cattle ranch. It is strange how life turns out, is it not,

25

Sergeant Saunders?" Augusta made a wry face as she spoke.

Brad nodded. Her story was but one of the many threads woven into the rich tapestry of life on the western frontier.

"But I am afraid that it is all about to change," she went on. "You see I am not an only child. Heinrich was my father's eldest son, but I have another brother, Willi, who is three years older than me. He also served in the Prussian Army, but in the commissariat. He came to America with us but refused to come out West. At first he worked for a shipping line in New York but then we lost touch until he arrived in Chanceville about a month ago. He had heard his father was seriously ill from one of his aunts back in Prussia. He has never been to visit his father. He spends his time gambling in Chanceville."

" . . . *waiting for him to die*," were the words she left unspoken, Brad surmised.

"And I take it he is expecting an inheritance?"

Augusta's lips tightened to a hyphen. "But of course. When we were children, my father always thought the world of Willi. In his eyes he could do no wrong."

"But what about you, ma'am?"

Augusta shot him a perceptive glance. She shrugged. "My future here is uncertain for I am sure that Willi will want to sell the ranch. He is in debt, I know that for certain."

"Have you discussed this with your father?"

Augusta shook her head.

"My father will not hear a word against Willi. But now, enough about my affairs, come, you will tell me how that man you have brought in came to be so badly treated."

Her eyes widened as Brad described the circumstances he had encountered earlier that day. Sensing that she was strong enough not to be fobbed off with a watered-down version, Brad left nothing out, including a description of how the sheep had been butchered in the pen.

As he spoke, he watched her closely, but he concluded that if she knew anything about this business he could find no evidence of it in her reaction.

"So, if he is a sheepherder," she said thoughtfully when he had finished, "he must be one of Lord Ewen's men."

Brad looked puzzled. "Lord Ewen?"

"Lord Ewen is an Englishman. He has come to Texas to raise sheep."

Brad winced. *Only an English lord would be crazy enough to do a thing like that.*

"Why Texas?" he demanded.

Augusta drew herself up. "Our families are old friends. They intermarried earlier this century. It was my father's suggestion that Lord Ewen come over from England to farm sheep."

Brad took a deep breath. "Surely your father must have been aware that sheep-raisin' ain't popular with cattlemen? After all, he's a cattleman himself."

"Excuse me, Sergeant Saunders, but you do not know my father. He is a businessman, he leaves the running of the ranch to the foreman. He is convinced that the future of this area lies in sheep rather than cattle."

Brad's eyebrows raised in surprise.

"And what makes him think that?" he enquired.

"He feels it is a mistake for Texas to raise one type of animal only — when the market fell three years ago, he lost a lot of money."

Brad nodded. "A lot of cattlemen went bankrupt."

"Well, my father, he survived. Had he been younger and in better health he would have brought in sheep himself."

"So what has happened since Lord Ewen arrived?"

Augusta sighed. "The cattlemen want him out. Morgan Holliger, who owns the Lazy Y, the biggest ranch in the county, invited him to a meeting of the

Cattleman's Association in Chanceville and told him so."

"Did you attend that meeting?"

Augusta nodded. "My father was too ill to go."

"And what exactly did Holliger say?"

"That it was impossible to raise both sheep and cattle together on the same land. Sheep spoil the grass by grazing it too close and leave an odour in the water holes which is distasteful to both cattle and horses."

Brad nodded. They were arguments with which he was familiar and he had never sought to question them.

"And how did Lord Ewen respond to that?"

"He said it was nonsense. He insisted that, with proper land management, sheep and cattle can be raised together, just as they are in Europe."

"But with respect, ma'am, this is Texas, not Europe."

Augusta nodded bleakly. "The problem is that when my father dies, Lord Ewen has lost a powerful backer."

"And from what I've seen this morning, it appears that someone is determined to force him out," Brad said. As he looked across at Augusta von Faulkenburg, her eyes met his and for a fleeting moment she looked drawn and vulnerable.

"Please don't think that I am involved, Sergeant Saunders," she said coldly. "It is no secret that there have been several unpleasant incidents involving a gang of masked men and Lord Ewen's herders of which this latest outrage you have just described to me is by far the worst. But whoever is responsible, none of them work at the Iron Cross, you have my word on that."

"I might say that I wasn't happy with the attitude of your foreman, Miss von Faulkenburg."

"Mr Pate has been a loyal servant to my father since the day he bought this ranch. He is not happy about having sheep in the area, he made that clear. I can understand his attitude, even

31

though I do not agree with it. But I assure you, he would have nothing to do with any campaign to get rid of Lord Ewen."

I only hope you're right! Brad thought grimly.

"What about this Morgan Holliger! Do you think he is capable of organizing a terror campaign to get rid of Lord Ewen?"

"Sergeant Saunders, there are several ranchers in the area who have strong feelings on the matter. Perhaps you had better question them," Augusta replied curtly.

It was plain she was not prepared to be drawn further on the subject of Morgan Holliger.

Which meant that it would require further investigation.

"Miss von Faulkenburg, let us both be quite clear on one thing. If that sheepherder dies, I'll be lookin' for the murderer."

Augusta looked at him coldly. "Sergeant Saunders, at that meeting in Chanceville, I made it quite clear that no matter how much I sympathized with the views of those present, I would never approve of any action against Lord Ewen which went outside the law."

"So threats of violence were made against Lord Ewen?"

"I did not say that!" Augusta flashed back.

Brad understood the situation well enough. He was well versed in the ways of cattlemen and his sympathies lay instinctively with them. The very idea of raising sheep here in the heart of Texas was an anathema to him.

"I guess I'll go have me a little talk with Lord Ewen," he said, rising to his feet.

"Will you, Sergeant Saunders?" For a brief moment Augusta von Faulkenburg's icy reserve broke down. "If only you could persuade Charles to give up this venture, there would be no more trouble, of that I am sure."

Her use of Lord Ewen's first name

was not lost on Brad. Was there something between them? If there was, he thought wryly, we could be heading for trouble piled on trouble.

"But what will your father think, Miss von Faulkenburg?"

"Leave my father out of this, he is a sick man," she snapped.

With that, she rose and Brad realized that his meeting with Augusta von Faulkenburg was over.

Brad's mood was thoughtful as he left the Iron Cross. Augusta von Faulkenburg was in a difficult position. Lacking her father's influential position as owner, she was clearly torn between denouncing the violence towards Lord Ewen and acquiescing to the wishes of the local cattlemen.

Brad had a strong feeling that, unless he was badly mistaken, Lord Ewen wouldn't give up that easily. After all, he thought, a guy doesn't come half-way round the world to start a business and then quit when the going gets tough.

3

"SO what's with the fancy duds?" Lee Holliger chaffed his brother as the latter strode into the stable yard of the Lazy Y. "Say, I got it, you're sparkin' fer her ladyship . . . "

Lee Holliger was five years younger than Morgan. In contrast to his brother's jet-black hair and neat grey suit he was blond as a Viking and so careless of his dress it was hard to believe the two shared the same parentage — but no one in the county ever dared question it except in darkened corners from behind the backs of their hands.

"Aw shut up," Morgan snarled. He flicked a speck of dust off his pants and adjusted the stock of his tie.

While they were talking, a rider entered the yard. He walked his horse over to the two men and dismounted.

"Morning, Mr Holliger," the man said.

Morgan recognized him as one of the clerks from the Cattleman's Bank in Chanceville.

"I've brought you a letter from Mr Brock," the clerk said.

Morgan froze inside. Frank Brock was the president of the bank. He wouldn't send this weasel-faced clerk with skin the colour of whey, who didn't know what a day's toil was, out on a special errand without good cause. He glanced at the man's face as he handed over the letter, and from the gleam in his eye, he guessed he knew the nature of the contents — he'd probably written it out himself.

"Thank you for your trouble," Morgan said. "Go see the cook for some coffee before you ride back."

"I'm obliged to you, Mr Holliger." The clerk touched his hat respectfully as he withdrew, leading his horse.

"Is there somethin' wrong?" Lee enquired, looking pointedly at the letter. "We're doin' OK aren't we?"

Morgan gave a curt nod before giving orders to the stable boy to have his horse ready in ten minutes and, followed closely by his brother, headed for the house.

Once inside, Lee gave a cavernous yawn. "Are we ridin' out tonight? I spotted another herder over by Pilson's Creek. We could take him out and run the critturs straight over the bluff — it'd save us the bother of killin' them."

"No. I reckon we'll wait and see what Ewen does, once he finds out what's happened this morning. Iffen he's any sense he'll clear out."

"You think so?"

When his brother didn't reply, Lee went on, "By the way, me an' the boys finished doctoring the herd for blowflies. It's been a bad year for 'em. It's a lousy job, the boys could sure use a break. Is it OK if they ride into town tonight?"

Morgan nodded. "Sure. I got a

meeting with Ezra Pate, an' then I'll ride on into town. Maybe I'll have me a hand at poker. Meantime I'll take a look at this letter."

His brother took the hint and left him. Morgan went into his office and closed the door.

Lines of well-thumbed files ran along a shelf. The heavy oak desk, used by his father, was strewn with unpaid bills. Morgan took a Havana cigar from a silver box, sliced off the end and lit it. Then he poured himself a generous shot of whiskey from a cut-glass bottle.

He slit the letter open with a paper-knife and as he read it his brow furrowed deep.

It was from Frank Brock, the President of the Chanceville Bank. Holliger's brow puckered as he read it.

The President regretted this and he regretted that, but under the circumstances, notwithstanding, and with due regard to . . .

The stock phrases rolled along the paper embellished with the fluency of the secretary's pen.

But in plain language, what it amounted to was that he, Morgan Holliger, the owner of the Lazy Y, owed the bank the sum of $31,344.20 and that nothing more would be forthcoming until the overdue payment of interest on the debt was met — and this payment was due within one month.

"What the hell am I gonna do?" Morgan muttered to himself as he pulled viciously at his cigar. "There ain't no way Frank Brock is gonna extend my credit. Looks like the Lazy Y has reached the end of the road."

He paced the office, deep in thought. The effect of the 1873 depression had bitten deep. Mounting debts had slowly but surely driven his father to suicide and sure as hell it was crippling him.

"Before Ewen came, I was makin' headway with Augusta von Faulkenburg," he figured. "She ain't no oil-paintin' but marriage to her would've solved my problems. Merging the two ranches would have staved off my bankruptcy. The baron surely would never have allowed the Lazy Y to go bust. But now the baron's gonna die and brother Willi's turned up, no doubt waiting for his inheritance . . . "

Morgan paused to consider the inch-long tip of ash which built up on the end of his cigar. Chances were the baron would leave the ranch to Willi and maybe settle a small annuity on Augusta.

What to do?

As sure as hell he wasn't going to go down without a fight. And he needed desperately to get this staging post deal under way with Ezra Pate.

For the last two years, the Iron Cross foreman had been secretly operating the Iron Cross as a link in a chain running rustled cattle north out of the Nueces valley. Under Baron von Faulkenburg's loose control, it had been easy for him to recruit suitable cowboys as henchmen, operate the ranch to the owner's satisfaction and promote his own operation.

A couple of months ago, when Morgan had discovered what Pate was up to, he'd figured a little blackmail might give him a lever over the guy, but Pate was smarter than that. He'd offered a partnership and the chance to expand the operation. At sixty-forty, Pate was driving a bargain, but Morgan needed his expertise. It was what is known in business parlance as the offer you can't refuse.

But what he desperately needed now was an injection of cash or securities to clear his debt and keep his legitimate business activity afloat — and soon.

Suddenly a possible solution to his problem came to him. Willi von Faulkenburg fancied his chances as a gambler, well maybe tonight was the time to put those ambitions to the test. If it meant staking all he had, then so be it. In the meantime he had this meeting fixed with Ezra Pate.

★ ★ ★

Augusta walked over to the window to watch the ranger leave. There was something decidedly mysterious about this quiet-spoken man; intuitively she realized that here was a man not to lie to or cross. He had questioned her with a persistence and tact that earned her respect, for she had found herself revealing far more than she would ever have allowed herself to do normally with a complete stranger. Her father had always had great respect for the Texas Rangers. It was perhaps fortunate for Pate that she had turned up when she did. But the thought the ranger had put into her mind bothered her: why had the foreman refused to allow the injured herder to be taken in?

There were several things about the way Pate ran the ranch which Augusta didn't understand. Since her father had fallen ill she had taken rather more interest in the day-to-day running of

42

the business than she used to, and it was obvious that Pate didn't like it. But that was only natural, she supposed. Even so, it was strange how he seemed to disappear completely for up to two or three hours sometimes. When he returned he always had some reasonable excuse.

She glanced at the long-case clock. It wanted ten minutes to noon. After she had eaten a light meal and changed there would be plenty of time to drive over to Lord Ewen's ranch and tell him about the misfortune which had befallen his sheepherder. And while she was about it, maybe she could persuade him to see sense . . .

The maid had laid out her afternoon clothes and Augusta changed out of her riding habit into a dress. Earrings and a neat brooch fastened round her throat with gold chain completed her ensemble.

An hour later Augusta drove the buggy through the gate and set off at a brisk trot along the trail which

43

led to the Chanceville road. Maria, the Mexican nurse, had assured her that her father was comfortable and that a few hours of complete rest would do him good.

As she left the track and turned onto the Chanceville road, she saw a lone rider heading towards her. At first she thought it was one of the hands but as he drew closer she saw that she was mistaken for he was too well-dressed. When they drew level, the rider reined in.

"Good afternoon, ma'am."

"Good afternoon, Mr Holliger."

Inside, Augusta felt a twinge of uneasiness at the man's cold appraisal. Morgan Holliger, the son of first-generation German immigrants had inherited his father's ranch twelve months ago, was a man of thirty, five years her senior. Tall, black-haired, broad-shouldered, dressed in a grey suit, he was a man highly aware of the impression created by his physical appearance. His face was clean shaven except for a neatly trimmed, fashionable, drooping moustache. The diamond and ruby pin in his neatly tied black stock winked in the sunlight. The butt of an ivory-handled revolver was just visible. The gleam of his polished riding boots was evident through a thin layer of trail dust.

Despite the brilliance of his smile and his smoothness of manner, Augusta trusted Morgan Holliger not a whit. From the day he'd had the effrontery to try to kiss her at a dance in Chanceville, instinctively she knew he was not the kind of man who ever did anything on mere whim.

"How is your father?" Holliger asked politely.

"He is not very well, I am afraid. There is no point in your stopping by, he will not be able to see you."

"Have you given further thought to my proposal?"

Augusta shivered inside. Morgan Holliger was a cold fish. Marriage wasn't something you discussed as impassively as a cattle deal.

"I have and my answer is still the same."

Morgan Holliger's expression changed. "Well now, it couldn't be that this has anything to do with that sheepherdin' Englishman?" he said angrily. "Why, I reckon you're goin' to visit him right now."

"I was not aware that my movements were any of your business," Augusta replied haughtily.

Morgan Holliger's wide smile narrowed. "Now you listen to me. Consorting with this man ain't gonna bring you nothing but grief . . . "

"Is that a warning?" Augusta flashed back.

"Take it any way you like. But I'm tellin' you that Lord Ewen's days around here are numbered. What are you thinkin' of? Your pa has a fine spread here. If he had any sense at all, he'd be on our side."

"My father is a sick man. He does not have long left to live. As for Lord

46

Ewen, I do not wish to discuss his affairs with you."

With that, Augusta shook the reins and moved away.

Holliger stared after the retreating buggy.

"So the old boy's ready to cash in his chips," he muttered to himself. His face broke into a sly smile. "Now just where is that gonna leave you, Miss High-and-Mighty, I wonder?"

★ ★ ★

Holliger could see Ezra Pate waiting for him in the shadow of the doorway of a cabin as he ran his horse into a small valley. Small groups of cattle were dotted here and there, grazing peacefully in the hot sunshine. Pate had chosen his location for a staging-post well.

The dying embers of a fire Pate had been using for his branding iron still radiated heat as Holliger dismounted. Two Iron Cross hands, who had been helping, took the opportunity to withdraw beyond earshot for a smoke.

"Howdy, Ezra, I've been talkin' with Augusta. It seems like the old buzzard is getting close to his last breakfast."

Pate shrugged. "Maybe. Look, that's the least of my worries. A guy's brought in that lousy sheepherder."

"So what?"

"He's still alive."

Holliger's expression became grim. "Alive, you say?"

Pate nodded. "An' the guy who brought him in is a ranger."

A chain of tiny beads of perspiration appeared on Morgan Holliger's brow.

"A ranger!"

The Iron Cross foreman mopped his sweating face with his bandanna.

"One of the servants overheard him talkin' to Miss von Faulkenburg. His name is Saunders."

"Saunders? You sure of that?"

Pate ejected a stream of tobacco juice.

"Sure."

"*Hell's teeth — Sergeant Saunders!*" Holliger ejaculated.

Pate's eyes narrowed. "D'you know him?"

"Yeah, I reckon he's one of McNelly's top men. It was him who busted King Solomon and his gang. Don't you remember? It was in the newspapers, 'bout six months back."

Pate stirred uneasily. "Christ, this whole business is startin' to stink . . . "

"Quit squawkin'," Holliger said. "We gotta think this through. How is it with the 'breed?"

"He ain't talkin', if that's what you're askin'. We should've hanged him straight off. That's the vigilante way. There was no need to make him watch us slaughter his sheep. He would've been dead if your brother had done the job properly."

Holliger stood away from the fence, his eyes hooding dangerously.

"Are you sayin' this is down to Lee?"

"So what? Are you wantin' to make something of it?"

For a moment the two men's eyes locked in a battle of wills.

Suddenly, Holliger relaxed. He looked up at the low hills surrounding them. "Ain't no use us fallin' out, Ezra, when we're gonna be partners," he said reasonably. "There's no need to worry about the herder. You were all wearin' masks. The guy would never recognize you. It's this goddam ranger we got to worry about."

Pate struck a lucifer on the fence-post to light the cigarette he had just rolled.

Holliger took out a chased silver flask from his hip-pocket. He unscrewed the top and took a long swig.

"I guess we'll have to do something about that ranger," he said bleakly.

"You mean get rid of him?"

"Sure."

Pate gave a low whistle, "That's a tall order, ain't it?"

"What's the matter? Don't you have the stomach for it?" Holliger jeered.

Pate flushed red.

"A sheepherder, maybe, but a ranger . . . "

"Can you think of a better idea?" Holliger went on remorselessly.

Pate shook his head. "Count me out. I'm still working rebranding this latest consignment."

"How long have you got?"

"It's gonna take two or three days yet. Miss von Faulkenburg's taking too much interest for my liking. I can only spare a couple of hours each day without being missed."

"We can't afford to let that ranger get in the way," Holliger said. "When he gets to Chanceville, he's gonna have a talk with the sheriff, that's fer sure. Having Ewen's sheepherders sniffin' round here is bad enough. The last thing we need is the law as well."

"Tex Grant don't want no trouble, that's fer sure," Pate mused. "But that ranger don't live here. He ain't one of us. He'll never find where we keep the cattle, it fooled you for long enough. He's bound to lean on Grant to take some kind of action. So what are we gonna do?"

"Like I said, we gotta get rid of him," Holliger said. "I reckon if I ride across country I could head him off and bushwhack him before he gets to Chanceville. How will I know him?"

"His hoss is a big bay stallion with a white blaze on his nose."

Holliger mounted his horse.

"You sure you're up to this?" Pate asked him. "Those ranger guys have got one hell of a reputation — you said it yourself."

"All any man needs is a bullet," Holliger said with a sneer. "Wish me luck."

Pate waited until Holliger had gone before he said through clenched teeth, "I reckon you're gonna need it, you arrogant bastard."

★ ★ ★

Lord Ewen was leaning on the post of the barn door, watching a Mexican shearing a fleece when Augusta turned the buggy into the yard.

There was bedlam in the fold nearby as a couple of hundred sheep, watched over by a herd-boy, milled around awaiting their turn to face the shearer's clippers and then take the plunge into the dipping tank.

A tall slim man, the sinews in Lord Ewen's bare forearms stood out like knotted cords as he helped her down.

"Augusta, how nice to see you. Do come inside."

Her face broke into smile as she warmed to him. "Thank you, Charles, I will."

Lord Ewen was about two years her senior and his cut-glass English accent and polished manners were a refreshing contrast to the rough and ready ways of western-bred men.

Augusta passed the reins of her horse to a smiling Mexican and paused, fascinated as the shearer dexterously finished clipping the fleece, and tossed it onto the pile behind him.

The house wasn't anything like the size of the mansion her father had built. It was a work-place, hastily constructed from timber and so crudely furnished and devoid of creature comforts that it made Augusta shudder at the spartan life led by its noble occupant used to the opulent family seat at which as a young girl she had once spent a month on a visit to England. She recalled how desperately she had fallen in love with this elegant youth who had grown into such an equally attractive man. But then she had been so young, and he too old to notice the anguish of calf-love . . .

But now the idealism of youth lay behind both of them, and as the youngest son of the Marquis of Granbury, it was no secret that Lord Ewen had nothing to inherit — and that meant he had to make his own way in life.

"You must forgive me, I'm not properly dressed. I wasn't expecting visitors," Lord Ewen said.

He rang a bell and a wizened-faced Chinaman wearing a white smock, appeared.

"Chiang is not as well trained as my father's butler," Lord Ewen said after he had ordered tea. "But he is very willing to learn; he finds the work more congenial than slaving on the railroads."

Augusta had to admit her formal dress and bonnet gave her the advantage over Lord Ewen's patched linen collarless shirt and the stained jodhpurs stuffed into a pair of dusty riding boots.

"Charles, I do apologize if the moment is not convenient," she said.

Lord Ewen held up his hands in mock horror. "As you see, we are in the midst of shearing." He nodded in the direction of the barn. "The revenue from selling these fleeces will set my business up nicely," he remarked good-humouredly. "Now tell me, how is your father?"

"Not good, I am afraid. The doctor says he has not got long to live."

"I'm very sorry to hear it, Augusta. He has been a great help to me. May I pay him a visit?"

Augusta shook her head. "He is not well enough. I am sorry, I have more bad news," she said, sipping her tea.

She spent the next few minutes recounting the events of earlier that day. By the time she had finished, Lord Ewen's expression was grave.

"Carlos isn't a 'breed," he said tersely. "He's a Basque. They are a proud people. If you suggested to him that he was of mixed blood, he would be mortally offended. I was expecting him to bring those sheep in for shearing later today. I was wondering where he'd got to."

Augusta shivered.

"Charles, what kind of men are they who would do such a thing?"

Lord Ewen shook his head. His mouth set to a hard line. "Whoever they are, they are determined to drive me out of here — and I am equally determined to stay."

"Perhaps the ranger will help?"

"Help?" Lord Ewen laughed harshly. "More likely he'll try to persuade me to leave. The rangers are certain to be on the side of the cattlemen. But let them do their worst. I'm breaking no law, I'm determined to stay."

Augusta stared at him. "One of your men is nearly killed, your sheep are slaughtered and you talk of carrying on?"

Lord Ewen met her gaze, determination in his steel-grey eyes.

"Augusta, let me make one thing quite clear. I'm not a remittance-man, here today and gone tomorrow. If I make a success of this venture, I have the promise of considerable financial backing from a Scottish-based investment company. So if you've been sent by the Cattlemen's Association as an emissary to persuade me to give up, then your journey has been wasted. No one is going to stop me."

Augusta rose to her feet, her face white with anger.

"If you think I am in any way involved in this matter . . . "

"My dear Augusta, I must confess I don't know what to think. Since the day I arrived I've met with nothing but hostility and downright interference. All right, I expected that, but this violence is the last straw. Right now I'm not inclined to trust anyone in the cattle business."

Augusta recoiled.

"Surely you trust me, Charles?"

Lord Ewen laughed bitterly. "After what you have just told me? Things have gone too far my dear Augusta. Don't you see? It's war from now on. And now, if you will excuse me I have work to do."

He ignored Augusta's furious expression, rose and rang the bell.

"Chiang, Miss von Faulkenburg is leaving now." He bowed to Augusta. "I will send a wagon over to collect Carlos. Goodbye."

Lord Ewen took a pipe out of his pocket and stuffed it with tobacco as he watched Augusta's departure.

"Chiang!" he shouted again as soon as she had gone.

The inscrutable butler appeared again mysteriously from within, like a genie from a lamp.

"Tell Raoul to saddle my horse," Lord Ewen snapped. "I'm riding into town."

4

BY the time Augusta arrived back at the Iron Cross, she had recovered her composure, and her first thought was for her father. She left the horse and buggy with Manuel and, without changing, went straight up to the sick room.

Maria, the Mexican nurse, rose as she entered. She put a finger to her lips and drew Augusta towards the door.

"*Cuánto lo siento, señorita*," she whispered. "But your father, he is not well . . . "

Augusta rushed over to the bed.

Baron von Faulkenburg lay propped on two pillows, skeleton-thin arms lying outside the sheet. His face was the colour of parchment and his breathing came in short wheezing gasps. As he turned his face towards Augusta, she saw from his expression that he knew he was facing his last struggle.

"Papa, how are you?" Augusta spoke to him in her native German as she always did as she sat down on a chair beside the bed.

"You are a good girl, Augusta," her father whispered. He looked pointedly at the nurse. "I wish to speak with you, alone."

The nurse did not speak German but at a nod from Augusta, she rose and left the room, her starched apron rustling.

"What is it, Papa?" Augusta said gently.

"Where is my Wilhelm?"

"He is still in town, Papa. He will come soon."

The baron regarded his daughter through half-closed lids.

"Willi has been my greatest disappointment," he murmured.

Augusta took her father's hand in hers and squeezed it gently; the hand that once had been so strong and powerful was now so weak it would not harm a fledgling.

"I am so sorry, Papa," she whispered. "I tried to persuade him to visit you, but he will not come."

"I know it is not your fault, child," came the reply. "And I am concerned about your future."

"Oh Papa, please do not worry about me."

"But you are not married. You should not have turned down Morgan Holliger."

"But I do not love him, Papa."

For a brief moment, Augusta quailed at the steely glint which flashed momentarily in her father's eyes.

"Love? What has love got to do with it?" he whispered. "In my day marriages were made to preserve dynasties, estates, fortunes . . . Morgan Holliger is of good Prussian stock . . . "

"Mamma loved you, she told me so," Augusta said stubbornly. "She did not marry you for any other reason."

"Did she say that? Thank you for telling me, my dear. It just shows how little you know the people who are nearest to you. Well, what's done is done. God bless you, my dear."

For a moment Augusta thought that her father had fallen asleep. But as she stole towards the door, he spoke again.

"Augusta!"

For a brief moment his voice sounded its old aristocratic, commanding self.

"Papa?"

"How is Charles faring?"

"It is difficult for him, Papa."

"I warned him it would be. But he is a very determined young man. Tell me, Augusta, does he show any regard for you?"

"I honestly cannot say, papa. But please do not concern yourself . . . "

"But I do care, Augusta. You cannot grieve forever. A fine young woman like you should be married."

"But I wanted to take care of you, Papa."

"Not for much longer, I fear. Promise me you will keep an eye on Willi, he is my only son . . . "

"Oh Papa, of course I will," Augusta cried as she bent over her father. Through eyes filling with tears, she saw his eyes close . . .

"Maria!" she called urgently. "Come quickly!"

The door opened and the nurse appeared. She hurried over to the bed and bent low over the emaciated figure, feeling for a pulse in the bony wrist. After what seemed an interminable length of time she straightened up. Her eyes met Augusta's and she shook her head sorrowfully.

★ ★ ★

Using his intimate knowledge of the country, Holliger spurred his mount on a course he figured would intercept the trail into Chanceville at a point ahead of the ranger. An hour's hard ride brought him to a small hill from the top of which he was able to see the trail winding towards him from some considerable distance.

From here, Pilson's Creek, which provided Chanceville and the surrounding area with water broadened out into a wide stream which ran alongside the trail. The landscape was dotted with grazing cattle and, lip curling in disgust, he spotted a flock of sheep about a quarter of a mile away.

Suddenly, to his immense satisfaction, he caught sight of a solitary rider approaching. All he needed to do was to get in close enough to verify the description of the horse Pate had given him and he had his man.

He eased his horse carefully off the bluff to avoid creating a cloud of dust and began to work his way towards the trail, using every possible scrap of cover to disguise his approach. So intent was he on his quarry, that he was unaware that he himself was being followed . . .

* * *

Diego Gonzales was a Mexican of diminutive proportions, whipcord thin and with a face, despite being protected by a sombrero, burned umber from exposure to many a summer's sun. As a humble pastor he kept watch over his flock of sheep as his family had done for generations.

Diego was a man of humble origins, a man without aspiration, but invested with dog-like devotion to any man who paid the small wage which kept his wife and children from the borders of starvation.

Dressed in his long coat, whatever the season, he kept his lonely vigil over his appointed flock. Diego's only companions for days on end were his Bible, his flock and his dog. Living constantly in the wilderness had given him an awareness of his environment as keen as that of the meanest insect that crawled God's earth.

And when the tall, well-dressed rider came into view, Diego spat so ferociously into a mesquite bush that half a dozen sheep paused to look at him with anxious eyes.

"Señor Holliger, if you have come to make trouble, then you shall have it," he said softly in his native language.

Diego walked over to his burro and reached for his gun. It was an ancient cap-lock breech-loader of the type made in the earlier part of the century. It was $52\frac{1}{2}$ inches long and weighed just over ten pounds. A hundred grains of powder fired a .52 diameter ball weighing half an ounce. He primed it with ten grains of fine powder.

Diego could not remember when he had last fired this weapon. It had been in his possession for many years. Family legend held that it had been fired in anger by his grandfather who was one of the forty Mexicans to escape from the battle of San Jacinto. But since Diego had come to work for Lord Ewen, attracted by the high wages, he had discovered that his new found prosperity had been bought at the possible price of his life.

By the time he had primed the flintlock, it dawned on Diego that he was not the focus of the approaching man's attention. Indeed, it appeared to him that his interest lay in another rider coming along the Chanceville trail.

Leaving his dog to guard the sheep, Diego moved on foot towards the trail, carrying the flintlock at high port. Of necessity his progress was slow, for he had to keep pausing to ascertain his quarry's intentions.

As Diego hit the trail, he became aware that the rider had halted and drawn his horse into a dry gulch. Out of the corner of his eye, Diego could see Holliger circling the site, a revolver in his hand. His target was obviously unaware of any danger as he unsaddled his horse and allowed it to roll whilst he set about gathering a few twigs of mesquite to light a fire.

It was quite clear to Diego that the would-be assassin, armed only with a revolver, was waiting for the man to sit down by the fire and present him with a motionless target.

Diego slid silently through the tangle of mesquite surrounding the gulch until he reached a point where he was on the opposite side to Holliger. He settled into a crouch with the flintlock against his shoulder. That moment would happen very soon, now.

Sweat coursed freely down Holliger's face as he crouched in the bushes on the edge of the gulch. The horse was indeed the big bay stallion with a white blaze, just as Ezra Pate had described it. His target was thus clearly identified.

But the business of getting in close enough to shoot the ranger had proved more difficult than he realized, for it would only take one dislodged stone to reveal his presence. He was within range now. All he had to do was wait until he had a stationary target. Once the water in the can came to the boil all the ranger's attention would be concentrated on brewing the drink.

As Brad waited for the water to boil, he rolled a smoke, mulling over the day's events.

The Iron Cross foreman's behaviour puzzled him. Pate's hostile reception convinced Brad that the man was involved in the campaign to get rid of Lord Ewen and his herders. Plainly, Augusta von Faulkenburg had not understood the reason for his hostility towards the man.

As Brad squatted on his haunches to make the brew, Blaze whickered.

Brad glanced round. The stallion was alert, his ears pricked up. The only thing that could make the stallion react this way was the close proximity of another horse.

Brad tensed, every sense alert.

The sharp snap of a twig in the undergrowth sounded a warning. A huge spurt of orange flame erupted from the mesquite bushes above him. It coincided with a rapid succession of gunshots and his tin mug was blasted several feet into the air showering him with droplets of scalding hot water.

Eyes closed, he leaped sideways, his hand clawing for his Peacemaker.

The silence following the noise of the guns was an almost tangible reality. Brad raised himself slowly upright, still wary, gun in hand, waiting for something to happen, but neither leaf nor insect stirred in the oven-hot gully.

Puzzled, he rose slowly to his feet. The droplets of water had burned his face, stinging like insect bites. As he stooped to recover his overturned coffee pot, a slight noise behind him made him whirl round.

The sight of a diminutive Mexican in a coat so long it almost brushed the ground, holding a flintlock of formidable proportions, did nothing to improve his humour.

"*Buenos dias, señor. Me llamo Diego Gonzalez.*" Brad slowly lowered his weapon.

"You must be one of Lord Ewen's herders?" he said, answering in Spanish.

The Mexican's mouth opened in a gap-toothed smile as he nodded.

"So what happened just now?" Brad demanded.

"*Señor*, you were being stalked by a man and I came to your aid. One shot from my gun was enough to send him away I think."

Brad looked at the still smoking musket barrel and nodded. He was highly conscious of the fact that but for the timely intervention of this little herder with his ancient flintlock, he would have suffered every ranger's nightmare and ended his days buzzard meat on the lonely range.

"Thank you," he replied. "But what made you think I was worth helping?"

Diego grinned. "Any man being stalked by another is worth helping. The honest man does not do his work on the sly."

"Have you any idea who it was?" Brad asked.

The Mexican shook his head. "I

do not know his name. But he is a cattleman."

Brad was puzzled. He had only just ridden into the area — how could someone be on to him already? The only people he had spoken to were the Iron Cross foreman and Augusta von Faulkenburg. A bead of sweat appeared on his forehead as realization hit him that she was the only person who knew he was a ranger.

"These are bad times, *señor*," Diego continued. "There is a group of vigilantes who are trying to drive us away. I have been warned to keep watch and be prepared for trouble."

Brad turned back his vest to reveal his badge of office.

"Ah, so you are one of the Texan Devils!" Diego's normally placid demeanour showed signs of agitation as he spoke. "Brought in by the cattlemen to get rid of us no doubt."

Brad accepted the herder's reaction with equanimity. He was well aware of the loathing which the very mention of the Texas Rangers roused amongst Mexicans.

"I work for no man, except my captain," he replied. "And let me make this quite clear: my job is to uphold the law. I have no authority to order either you or your employer to leave the county."

"But I do not understand. Why should a cattleman want to kill you?"

"That is what I aim to find out," Brad replied tersely.

"Perhaps we can find out in which direction the man has fled," Diego said helpfully.

The two men searched the area together and rapidly came to the same conclusion.

"He has ridden into town," Diego said.

"And once there, his tracks will be lost in a hundred others," Brad said.

"I am sorry I cannot be of more help, *señor*. But you understand I spend all my time on the range with my sheep."

Brad nodded. "Tell me, would you be prepared to testify against any of these men who have threatened you?"

The little herder's expression became apologetic.

"How can I, *señor*? I have a wife and family to keep. You know how it is."

★ ★ ★

The shock of being fired at from the opposite side of the gulch took a few seconds to register with Morgan Holliger. As soon as it did, he made a hasty retreat to his horse, leapt into the saddle and made off along the trail to Chanceville as fast as the animal would carry him.

It took nearly an hour of hard riding before he was fully convinced that no one was following him. He slowed his horse down for the final few miles in order to compose his thoughts.

His attempt to kill the ranger had failed. Miserably, it seemed, until he considered the fact that right up to the moment when he had his gun trained at the ranger, he was as good as dead, until someone else had intervened.

Whoever it was had fired some kind of primitive musket at him, for the ball had whistled past him with a terrifying sound, ripping through leaves and branches as it went by.

The unwholesome truth was that he himself had been followed by someone who had spotted him trailing the ranger.

Now who could that be?

The answer dawned on him as he arrived at the outskirts of Chanceville. The only man whom he'd seen since leaving Ezra Pate was one of Ewen's sheepherders about a quarter of a mile away from the gully. All Ewen's herders carried weapons — many of them of ancient vintage.

Would the man have recognized him? Holliger shrugged. What did it matter if he did? No one would believe a word uttered against him by a lousy sheepherder, that was for sure — he had no worries on that score.

He rode past a circus setting up camp on the outskirts of town, and headed for Weaver's Hotel, the best hotel in Chanceville. The owner was Hank Weaver, a local businessman, who would be at tonight's poker game.

Holliger left his horse at the livery barn, checked in with the clerk and booked a room for the night.

"Would you like a bath, sir?" the clerk enquired.

Holliger glanced sharply at the man. But if he was passing an overt comment on his guest's somewhat dishevelled appearance, the man was too astute to reveal it.

A couple of hours later, Holliger reappeared in the foyer, his skin glowing from the hot bath the maid had drawn for him and the extra services she had willingly provided for the money he had offered.

His clothes were neatly brushed and his hair slicked down. By this time the debacle of the afternoon was now just a memory. When the ranger arrived in town (and he had no doubt that he would come) there would doubtless be another opportunity to get rid of him.

In the meantime, there was the little matter of relieving Willi von Faulkenburg of his inheritance.

He walked down the steps of the hotel with the jaunty air of a man-of-the-world.

For every man who gambles, there is always another day — provided he survives to tell the tale.

5

IT was early in the evening for drinking, but Willi von Faulkenburg, fashionably dressed in a superbly tailored grey suit and flower patterned vest, was already standing with one highly-polished Spanish leather boot fixed firmly on the brass foot rail of the bar of the gambling hell they called the Graveyard Saloon, his eyes staring fixedly at a glass of whiskey.

Despite its macabre name, it was the proud boast of the owner that his business was in the forefront of the type of service it provided for the residents of Chanceville. Indeed, Carter Rankin would have taken issue with anyone who voiced an opinion that the 'margaritas' (as he euphemistally called them) he employed were not of the highest class and that the gambling facilities on offer were without parallel anywhere between Chanceville and New York.

Given his superior knowledge of what he considered to be the more sophisticated life in Europe, Willi chose not to pass comment.

"Is Mr Holliger coming in tonight?" the barman asked affably as, without needing to be asked, he topped up Willi's cut-glass tumbler.

Willi nodded. Albeit uncomfortably. A forced smile illuminated his thin features momentarily, but inside, his guts were beginning to churn.

He already owed $10,000.

Christ! Whatever had made him think that these guys out West couldn't play a decent game of draw poker?

He tried to banish the thought, but sweat spurted in his forearms at the thought of how in less than one month of sitting in at the tables, his IOUs had mounted steadily. Never in his life had he experienced such a run of bad luck except that which had led to his dismissal from the shipping line. Back in New York, gambling debts and the threat of strong-arm methods for their recovery had led him to 'borrow' from the firm's accounts. Only by a piece of sheer good fortune involving the misplaced devotion of the owner's daughter and the ability to lie fluently and travel light had kept him from hearing the metallic clang of the prison door.

$10,000!

Any day Chanceville's gambling fraternity could choose to call that debt in. If they did, he was in deep trouble. He had a funny feeling that they were playing him like a fish on a line.

But there was a ray of hope. Praise be the old man was sick. With any luck he would die soon, and when he inherited the ranch, his troubles would be over. Not for Willi the hard graft of raising longhorns; from what he'd seen in this brief foray out West, they were nasty, smelly cantankerous creatures. The money made from the sale of the ranch would pay his debts, leaving enough to invest in the shares of a Mississippi river boat company. After that, no more gambling. Absolutely no more; never again . . .

"Here he comes now."

Willi turned round slowly on the barman's words to face Morgan Holliger. The latter paused as he emerged through the batwings savouring the effect his arrival created. His bone-headed brother, Lee, was in tow, sporting a grin as wide as a kid at the prospect of going to the circus.

"Shall we go up!" Holliger said when he saw Willi.

"Sure," Willi replied. He kept his voice low and casual although inside he felt like a man going to the condemned cell.

When they reached the foot of the staircase Morgan said to his brother, "Push off, kid."

"Aw, can't I come and watch?"

"No." Morgan flipped out his wallet and peeled off a handful of notes. "Go have yourself some fun," he indicated the gaming tables at the far end of the room as he spoke.

"Come on, honey, I'll help you spend it."

A garishly painted margarita, long past her vintage years, with an over-painted face and under-dressed in a low-cut, cheap, red gown, skilfully simulated a provocative pout as she slipped her arm through Lee's.

"I didn't say all at once," Morgan said, with a contemptuous smile as he mounted the staircase.

"Hello, boys, nice seein' you!"

Carter Rankin sprang forward out of the shadows at the top of the stairs like a spider from the corner of his web. He was dressed in a dark suit with a silver watch chain sprawled across his fat belly. He sported a clutch of chunky gold rings like knuckledusters on each of his fingers. His greeting was always uttered with the same sly smile; the way a hangman might smile if he were allowed to catch his victim's eye . . .

Morgan greeted the saloon owner with a curt nod.

"Well now, boys, I guess I got a real nice clientele here tonight. I got Alabama Rose in, too . . . "

Rankin's lips curled back in a soundless snigger as a grunt came from behind the closed door of the room they were passing.

" . . . that is, when she's through with Mr Tuttle."

Willi winced. Everard Tuttle was a large man, with a matching appetite for the fleshly pleasures. In between indulging these, he was the family lawyer. Rumour had it he intended to present himself as a candidate for the State Legislature at the next election.

They reached the door to a suite of rooms. A one-eyed, scar-faced, gap-toothed, pot-bellied doorman with an expression akin to a bored prison warder, stood aside deferentially to allow the men to enter.

It was another of Rankin's proud boasts that within the expensively papered walls of the suite, fitted with oriental carpets and illuminated by a series of matching crystal glass chandeliers, no woman had ever set foot and any kind of gambling game could be played. Full-length gilt mirrors strategically placed on the walls enhanced the impression of size.

In the first room, through a cloud of rich-smelling cigar smoke, a croupier's voice droned, *"Faites vos jeux . . . "*

The only other sound was the click of the ball as it whirled round and round . . .

Passing through, they came to the billiard room. Both tables were occupied and none of the shirt-sleeved, eye-shaded players bequeathed them a second glance. Beyond this lay the holy of holies — a small room, as sumptuously furnished as the ante-rooms and with just enough space to comfortably fit a card table and up to eight players.

"Howdy."

Willi nodded affably to the four men

who were already absorbed in a game of draw poker. Three of them were cattlemen. The bull-necked Jackson Venn was a rancher with a reputation for not suffering fools gladly. He numbered the Baron von Faulkenburg and Lord Ewen amongst these. Lance Quirk, whose steel-rimmed spectacles gave him a curiously academic air which belied his reputation for hard-dealing, ran a transport business — his wagons brought all the goods and supplies into the area. The astute, urbane Hank Weaver, owned a number of businesses in Chanceville, including the best hotel in town.

The joker in the pack was the grey-haired, patrician Frank Brock, President of the Cattleman's Bank.

Taken together, this group of men from such diverse backgrounds, formed a formidable array of gambling talent.

The sight of the cards cascading on to the green baize set the blood racing in Willi's veins. As the fever took him, he was possessed with the consuming thought that this would be his lucky night. Later, when he rose from the table, free of debt, these men would look at him as an equal and with the respect that ought to be accorded a baron's son and the rightful inheritor of the Iron Cross.

"I take it you two want in!" Jackson Venn asked pleasantly, rolling a Havana cigar round his yellow teeth as he spoke.

"Sure," Willi replied.

"Welcome to the pot," Quirk said. "Brandy?"

And Willi sat down like a lamb in front of a pride of hungry lions . . .

★ ★ ★

The sun was poised like an orange disc balancing on the horizon when Lord Ewen rode along Chanceville's main street. Sheriff Grant looked up sharply when he entered his office. He had the strained look of a man at the end of his tether.

"What do you want?" Grant snapped.

"Good evening, Sheriff," Lord Ewen replied courteously.

"Cut the fancy talk. I asked what do you want?"

"Nothing except the return of common politeness and the freedom to raise my sheep," Lord Ewen said evenly.

Grant eased his bulk out of his swivel chair. He was still a good-looking guy although his thinning hairline and a bulge about his waist indicated the onset of middle-age. Like many of his fellow westerners he mistook Lord Ewen's impeccable manners for effeteness and he made no attempt to disguise the look of contempt on his scowling face.

"Listen, Ewen, I told you right from the start that bringing sheep here would come to nothing but grief."

"You were certainly right about that, Sheriff."

"Does that mean you're pullin' out?" Grant asked hopefully.

Ewen shook his head and Grant

listened in silence as Ewen recounted what Augusta von Faulkenburg had told him earlier that day.

"I've been to see for myself," Ewen concluded. "I estimate I've lost two hundred and ten head of sheep. And not only that, Carlos, one of my herders, has been flogged almost to death and what is more, his assailants attempted to kill him."

He took out a packet of cheroots and offered them to Grant, who refused, preferring to roll a smoke of his own. Ewen selected one and lit it, and blew a series of smoke rings towards the ceiling.

"So may I ask what you are going to do about it, Sheriff?" he enquired.

Grant sat back and stared at the slim, unarmed man standing in front of him.

He's like a lamb to the slaughter.

He found it difficult to dismiss the uncomfortable metaphor from his mind, for whatever he thought personally about sheep, it was clear a serious crime had been committed. To his intense annoyance he had to admit that Ewen was right; it was his job to investigate it.

"Well?"

"Now see here, it ain't as cut and dried as you're makin' it out to be," Grant replied. "Cattle raisin' is the nat'ral way of doing things out here. To a rancher, the sight of a sheep is like wavin' a red cape in front of a Spanish bull. When guys like you come along, the cowman is gonna fight tooth and nail to keep what he knows and understands."

"But the law . . . "

"The law be danged!" Grant shouted, his face purple with rage. "Now see here, Ewen, I got more'n enough on my hands dealin' with every kinda trouble in this town without you addin' to it." He rose and walked over to the window. "There's a circus arrived an' it looks like the entire population of the county is arrivin' in town. In a couple hours I'm gonna have a whole heap of problems out there."

"But help is at hand," Lord Ewen said quietly. "Miss von Faulkenburg told me a Texas Ranger was first on the scene. I gather he's on his way. Hasn't he arrived yet?"

Grant's face changed. "A ranger, you say? Why the hell didn't you tell me that, first off?" His expression became crafty. "Why, I guess you were figurin' me out, weren't you?"

"I must say I can't say I blame you for taking the line you do," Lord Ewen replied reasonably. "After all it is you who has to deal with these people. But perhaps it would be better if you put the matter of finding the gang that is terrorizing my sheepherders into the hands of another lawman."

Grant flushed red at the studied implication in Ewen's remark, but he kept a rein on his temper.

"Well I'm tellin' you, mister, I ain't seen no ranger hereabouts."

Lord Ewen shrugged enigmatically. "Maybe he's got held up on the way.

Look, it's been a long ride in, I think perhaps I'll pop over the road to a hostelry and have a drink. Perhaps you'll let me know as soon as he arrives?"

Sheriff Grant shook his head in wonderment as Lord Ewen strode out of his office.

"Pop over the road to a hostelry and have a drink? He's mad," he muttered. "Stark, starin', ravin' mad."

★ ★ ★

Dusk was gathering when Brad rode into Chanceville. He smiled when he saw Dolly Bailey's travelling circus had set up a three-pole tent alongside the stream just outside the town. Around it a small town of wagons and tents had sprung up. The lady herself was taking the air, with a little dog in attendance, as he drew level with the entrance.

"Howdy, Brad! Nice seein' you."

"Howdy ma'am," Brad tipped his hat to the smiling woman who stepped out of the shadows. "You sound like you've been expectin' me."

Dolly Bailey was one of the toughest women Brad had ever met in the West. Built as solidly as a prizefighter, legend had it she had once floored a casual hand with a punch smack on the jaw for teasing one of the tigers.

"My lion-tamer saw you ridin' north outa San Antonio."

"News travels fast," Brad said with a smile.

"Sure does. Bye-the-bye, you can quit the ma'am, boy, my name's Dolly to you."

Brad grinned as he grabbed an eyeful of cleavage as deep as a canyon. Not many people were allowed to call her by her first name. Dolly ran her circus with all the panache of a South American dictator and her sexual appetite was said to be legendary. What would the West be like without characters like her?

"I was just being polite, I guess."

"Too polite fer me. I can't understand why a guy like you ain't married to a nice girl like me and we ain't raising a couple kids on some nice spread."

"That'll be the day."

Brad caught the knowing twinkle in her eye and they both laughed.

"Says you. Let me know when you're ready. You got business in town?"

"Reckon so."

"Well now, you take my advice. Chanceville's a real mean town. There's a fuse burning just like it's gonna blow sky high. I've travelled too much not to notice these things. I've put it off-limits for my crew. You take care of yourself, boy. You hear me?"

"I hear you, Dolly."

"We open tomorrow. Remember, there's always a seat for you," Dolly called after him as he moved on.

Brad acknowledged her with a wave and he disappeared into the darkness, Dolly Bailey stood watching him, hands on hips, her bosom heaving.

There goes a real man, she thought.

As he rode past the wagon-park, one of the circus acts, a juggler, recognized

Brad and waved acknowledgement. For a few moments, the air was full of the rank smell of predators. In the gloom he caught sight of a tiger pacing to and fro inside its cage and the spine-tingling roar of a lion made the usually even-tempered Blaze skittish.

Chanceville was a much bigger town than he had expected, which accounted for its place on Dolly Bailey's itinerary. It was laid out geometrically with side streets leading off a broad, central, tree-lined avenue. A dust devil on the rising night-wind sent trash spinning along the main street. In answer to his question, an old-timer, puffing at an evil-smelling pipe, directed him past a dry goods store in the direction of the sheriff's office.

"But don't you count on finding him there, son. He's kep' mighty busy these days — 'specially come sundown. Hope you ain't a preacher-man, fer Sodom an' Gomorrah ain't got nuthin' on this town. Heh, heh, heh!"

Brad nodded his thanks and rode on.

The deeply rutted road ran past a line of dwellings backing on to the stream. They were fronted by neat gardens with flower borders and wicket fences and suddenly gave way to a board walk and a miscellany of stores, saloons and cheap lodging-houses. The town was big enough to warrant an enginehouse, the big doors of which were open to reveal the polished brasswork of the fire engine with its hose cart and reel standing beside it.

The noise level from the saloons was already high and several cowhands, already the worse for drink, were arguing in loud voices. From the far end of an alley came the shouts and curses from the spectators gathered at a cock-fight.

The sheriff's office stood somewhat apologetically between the pretentiously named Parisienne Clothing Emporium and a saddler's shop. It was, as he had been led to expect, empty; no doubt Tex Grant was out on his rounds.

"You lookin' fer the sheriff, mister?"

Brad looked down at the ragged-assed urchin who addressed him.

"Know where I might find him, boy?"

"Maybe."

Brad grinned at the laconic answer. The kids these days had old heads on young shoulders. He flipped him a quarter.

The urchin's Rabelaisian features brightened as he caught the coin deftly.

"Reckon you might find him at the Graveyard Saloon," he said with a cheerful grin. "It's yonder side of Cockpit Alley. Could be trouble there, I reckon. Me, I'm off to take a look-see."

Brad shook his head in wonderment as the urchin hopped and skipped like a Jack-o'-lantern into the night.

He dismounted outside a livery stable and left Blaze with the lad. He would find a hotel later after he'd finished his business with the sheriff.

The night was becoming sultry as

Brad eased his Peacemaker in its holster and mounted the boardwalk. He had scarcely taken four paces towards the saloon when suddenly, two shadowy figures lurched out at him. When he regained his balance, Brad found one of the men was pointing a gun somewhere between his belly and the ground and the other was holding a knife, albeit somewhat shakily, at his throat.

"Let's have your wallet, mister."

It was the man holding the knife who spoke. His words were slurred and his face was so close to Brad's, he caught the sour smell of whiskey on his breath.

Irritated rather than angry with the delay caused by this pair of bunglers, Brad brought his right elbow backwards with all his force. It sank deep into the belly of the man holding the knife. As he doubled over retching and gasping, all the breath expelled from his lungs, Brad dove forward, knocking his companion's gun away with a chopping movement; simultaneously he brought his knee up and smashed it into the man's crotch. The man howled in agony as he slumped backwards against the wall.

Oblivious to the havoc he had wreaked, Brad stooped to pick up the knife and gun aware as he did so that the passers-by were stepping over the writhing bodies of the two men as though nothing had happened.

As he straightened up, he heard the sound of a gunshot from the saloon.

The old-timer was right. It looked like Sheriff Grant had his hands full . . .

6

IN the short while he had been in the area, Lord Ewen had only ventured into Chanceville a couple of times during the daytime to collect supplies and so the din inside the Graveyard Saloon came as something of a surprise to him. To his vast amusement, it appeared that the quiet, respectable town of the daylight hours turned by nightfall into a Dickensian den of iniquity.

"What's your poison, mister?" the barman asked him as he strode up to the bar.

"Whiskey, my man," Lord Ewen replied.

"Give him Sheep's Piss, Jake," a loud, mocking voice said.

"What's that?"

Lord Ewen turned round as he spoke.

"I said Sheep's Piss. Just the swill fer a scab herder."

"Excuse me, old boy," Lord Ewen said. "But there's no cause for you to call a chap names."

"Excuse me, old boy!" the man mimicked Lord Ewen's accent to a T.

"Back off, Lee," the barman said as the chorus of laughter subsided.

Lee Holliger's thin lips curled into a sneer. "Back off? Not on your life. Not while this scab herder's here in town."

He spat on his hands and rubbed them together. "Know what I'm gonna do? Why I'm gonna throw him outta here, neck an' crop . . . "

Lee Holliger's words died as he attempted to lay hold of Lord Ewen for the latter's crisp jab caught him full in the mouth, crushing his lips against his teeth. The blow threw him off balance so that he fell backwards over a table which collapsed under his weight, scattering the occupants, their drinks, cards and poker chips in a volley of startled curses.

Lee shook his head, his hand pawing at the ooze of blood which spurted down his chin from his cut lip. As he slowly rose to his feet, the saloon fell silent.

"Well now, scab herder, if you wanna fight, you got one," he said.

"Go on, Lee, give him a good hidin'," an onlooker shouted to a roar of approval.

"Smash him, Lee!" shouted another.

As he lunged forward, slinging a wild haymaking right, Lee was vastly surprised to find his opponent inside it, jabbing him painfully on the nose twice before floating tantalizingly out of reach again.

"Come on and fight!" Lee shouted, blood now pouring from his broken nose.

"That's just what I am doing," came the calm reply.

Lee stared at Lord Ewen like a baffled bronc, tormented by his breaker. His adversary had adopted a strange posture, his right hand was guarding his chin and the left extended forward in the manner of a prize fighter.

Lee's next rush was as unproductive as the last; Ewen danced in and out and round and round, catching him off-balance peppering his face and body with a series of accurately timed punches which stung like hell.

Aware of the jeers of the crowd, Lee saw red. He put his head down and charged forward, only to be picked off by a beautifully timed right uppercut which sent him flying on to his backside amid hoots of laughter.

"Give in, Lee, boy, give in! You've been bested!" a massive teamster shouted. It was an opinion endorsed by all present.

Enraged at his loss of face, Lee's hand went for his Colt.

"Hold it right there."

Everyone's attention was drawn to the harsh command which came from the doorway.

"Throw down that gun, Lee, the

fun's over," Sheriff Grant said as he strode into the centre of the room. He was carrying a Spencer carbine, of Civil War vintage, tucked in the crook of his arm.

"No!" Lee shouted, his face white with anger.

"Come on, boy, we don't want any trouble, do we?" Grant said. "Drop your gun and I'll forget about the fight."

"No doubt you will," Lord Ewen said evenly.

"You shut up," Grant snapped. "I've seen enough of you for today."

But Lee was too far gone down the road of humiliation to return to reason.

"Back off!" he shouted.

"Lee, don't make me have to arrest you."

As Sheriff Grant took a further step forward, Lee Holliger raised his weapon and fired . . .

* * *

At the sound of the shot, Brad left his two erstwhile attackers writhing in agony on the boardwalk and ran with giant strides towards the pool of yellow light which bathed the entrance to the bullet-riddled skull and crossbones sign which proclaimed the entrance to the Graveyard Saloon.

As he pushed open the batwings and entered, the silence inside was as tangible as the noise which only a moment or two earlier had affronted his hearing.

He took in the situation at a glance. The acrid whiff of gunsmoke overlaid the amorphous smell of sweat, tobacco smoke and cheap perfume. The body of a man lay slumped on the floor. Ten yards beyond another man was locked in a gunfighter's crouch with his back to the bar. The wisp of smoke rising from his gun, was coalescing with the blue haze of tobacco smoke which hung in a cloud round the fancy gilt chandeliers. The floor was littered with spilled drinks, poker chips and overturned chairs and tables.

Brad was the only moving figure in a waxen-faced tableaux of gamblers, cowboys, small-town businessmen and soiled doves. He felt his anger rise for the second time that day as he stooped to look at the prostrate figure. The silver star pinned to his shirt told him it must be Tex Grant, the Sheriff of Jameson County. The rivulet of blood pumping from the hole in his shoulder showed he was wounded.

Squatting on his heels, Brad's eyes swept over the assembled company before coming to rest on the gunman. He was no more than a kid, flushed with the taint of gunplay. Probably his first . . .

"He never gave me a chance," Grant whispered. "I guess I must be losin' my touch." Before he could say more, his head slumped to one side in a paroxysm of pain.

"You hear that?" Brad said, his voice low and full of menace.

"He's a liar!" Lee Holliger's voice

rose a notch. "He came in totin' a gun. It was self-defence. Anyone here will tell you that. Anyway, what's it to you, mister? It ain't none of your business."

"That's where you got it wrong, boy."

As he spoke Brad drew back his vest to reveal his badge of office.

"Christ, he's a ranger!" an awed voice broke the silence.

"Right," Brad agreed. "An' I don't take kindly to a fellow lawman being called a liar." He turned to Lee Holliger. "I'm arresting you, boy, for attempted murder."

The young man's thin features broke into a crooked smile.

"Now how you gonna do that, seeing as I've got the drop on you?"

"I'm givin' you the chance to give yourself up," Brad said. "Don't pass it up twice in one day."

"Act smart, kid," a voice called. "You're outa your depth. Tangle with a ranger and you'll have McNelly's company after you like a swarm of bees."

But even as the voice spoke, Brad saw the barrel of the gun moving upwards and he was uncoiling like a released spring out of his crouch sideways to his left. At the same instant his right hand moved in one fluid movement for his Peacemaker.

The roar of the explosions from both weapons sounded as one. The difference was that Lee Holliger's weapon was pointing at the spot where Brad had been a split-second previously and Brad's was pointing directly at him.

There were two belches of merging gunsmoke and he heard a woman scream. His adversary slammed back against the bar and, holding both hands to his head, slumped slowly to the floor. Brad rolled over once and remained flat on his belly, prepared to fire again if necessary.

When nothing happened, he rose slowly to his feet, holding his Peacemaker at the ready, aware of the excited babble that had broken out amongst the spectators. From behind the bar, Jake the barman's bald, sweating dome rose like the sun slowly over the horizon.

Brad bent down over Lee Holliger. The bullet from his Peacemaker had grazed the side of his head. To his relief, he began to stir.

"Reckon you could be in big trouble, Ranger," the barman called out. "You just done shot Morgan Holliger's kid brother."

"He made the first move," a quiet voice said. "I'll vouch for that."

"Who are you?" Brad asked.

"I am Lord Ewen."

Brad stared at the slim Englishman. "What the hell are you doin' here?" he demanded.

"I called to see Sheriff Grant and came in here for a drink while I was waiting for you."

Brad shook his head in wonderment.

"Make way fer the doc!" a voice called out.

"You'd best come along with me to the sheriff's office after I've dealt with this," Brad told Lord Ewen.

Doc Kearnsey was a tall, round-shouldered man. Steel-rimmed glasses perching precariously on the end of a great beak of a nose gave him a permanently inquisitive expression. His frayed black suit, stained with all kinds of unimaginable horrors, hung loosely on a gaunt frame almost as devoid of flesh as the skeleton which dangled in a gloomy recess of the office to which, after a cursory examination of his patients; he had them transferred with an efficiency which belied his grotesque appearance.

In five minutes he had shaved the hair away from the graze on the still dazed Lee Holliger's scalp, doused it liberally with iodine and covered it with a bandage. Then while Brad made to take his prisoner to the jail, he stripped off his jacket and commenced an examination of Grant's wounded shoulder with deft movements of his prehensile fingers.

"Six inches this way and you'd have been a cadaver," he said, shaking his head mournfully.

"Well, don't sound so danged disappointed," Grant said.

"I'm gonna have to cut the bullet out. Guess you ain't gonna be much good at sheriffin' fer a while."

"I'll go along with that," Brad agreed. "Tex, it seems like I'd best take over. But there's some things I gotta know about."

"You done talkin', mister?" Doc Kearnsey interrupted. "Or do I have to cut your tongue out to get some peace and quiet?"

Brad backed away at the sight of the doctor bearing down on him with a scalpel.

"Some other time, I guess," Brad said, backing towards the door. "By the way Doc, I got another patient for you out at the Diamond T. He's one of Lord Ewen's sheepherders."

"What's wrong with him?"

"He's been flogged half to death and shot."

"So I take it I can rely on you for a steady flow of patients from now on, Sergeant Saunders?"

Brad quailed under Doc Kearnsey's saturnine stare and made good his escape.

As he stepped out into the street holding the sullen Lee Holliger at gunpoint, he became aware of a crowd gathering outside the sheriff's office. Their hostility was self-evident. Brad's main concern was to get his prisoner under lock and key.

"There he is!" a voice shouted.

"Hold it, mister."

"Who are you?" Brad demanded of the big, well-dressed man who stepped forward to confront him.

"Me? I'm Morgan Holliger, the brother of the man you got here with you."

"Well, he's under arrest for attempted murder," Brad said. "I'm takin' him to jail."

"What for?"

"So he can face trial."

Morgan Holliger's shout of laughter led the general mirth which spread like a prairie fire amongst the onlookers.

"If you think you can make a charge like that stick," Holliger said, "you gotta surprise comin'. No jury in this county would ever convict a Holliger — certainly not on the word of a lousy sheepherder."

"Best come into the office and we'll discuss it in private," Brad said.

"No," Holliger said. "What I got to say can be said out here."

"OK," Brad replied evenly. "Say it."

"I am one of the biggest cattlemen in this county," Morgan Holliger blustered. "I am President of the Cattleman's Association. I'm tellin' you that if you don't release my brother right now, there's gonna be hell to pay."

"You should've saved your breath," Brad advised.

"Save yours, Ranger, while you still got some."

Brad resumed his journey to the sheriff's office with Lee Holliger.

"I am still prepared to make a statement," a voice said behind him as he entered the office.

Brad turned to find Lord Ewen standing in the doorway.

Once inside, Brad lit a lamp, locked his prisoner in a cell and then rounded on Ewen.

"What the hell are you still doin' in town?" he demanded. "Haven't you caused trouble enough for one night?"

"I beg your pardon," Lord Ewen replied. "But I didn't start the fight. I came originally to ask the sheriff for protection from those who are trying to create trouble for me."

"Instead, you made matters a sight worse," Brad snapped. "Well, my advice to you is to get the hell outa here until I get things under control."

"Do you really think you can do that after what has just happened?" Lord

Ewen said quietly. "The townsfolk are dead against you, that's clear enough."

"Thanks to you," Brad said sourly.

"Now, wait a minute. You have no right to accuse me of causing trouble. I have just offered to be a witness . . ."

"Forget it," Brady snapped. "There ain't no way a jury will listen to you. If you stay here, I can't guarantee your safety."

As he spoke, the office was suddenly lit by an eerie orange glow.

He walked over to the window and peered outside. Beyond the boardwalk was a score of men each of whom were wearing crude masks made out of gunny sacks and holding a flaming torch in his hand.

"You hear me, Saunders?"

There was no mistaking the voice of Morgan Holliger, although it was impossible to detect him in the group.

"You let Lee Holliger go free now or we're gonna come in and get him and Ewen as well!"

7

"IT looks as though we might have a problem," Lord Ewen reflected mildly.

Brad ignored him, his mind was too busy considering the situation. Grant's office fronted the jail and was lit by a single window protected by a grille of iron bars. Brad realized immediately that once the glass was broken there was no place invulnerable to direct fire or the ricochet of a spent bullet except the interior of one of the cells.

In short, the place was a death trap to any would-be defender in the face of a determined attack.

"One thing is certain, we can't stay here," Lord Ewen said mildly.

The Englishman's composure was amazing. But one thing was certain; for a ranger to give up a prisoner voluntarily was unthinkable.

Brad glanced sharply at Lord Ewen. "Can you handle a gun?"

"I was brought up on my father's country estate. He would have been cross had I failed to acquire the facility to bag a few brace of grouse," came the reply. "Besides which I did serve for ten years in the Lancers."

"Come on, Ranger, we're waitin'!" Holliger shouted. "You hand over my brother and get outa town with that scabherder. That's the only deal you're gonna get."

"You hear that?" Lee Holliger shouted from the cell. "You'd best do as my brother says or you're gonna die."

Brad ignored him as he snatched up the bunch of keys. He tossed them to Lord Ewen.

"One of 'em should fit the gun rack. Grab yourself a weapon — quickly!"

Even as Lord Ewen fiddled with the keys, the first volley of shots smashed through the barred window showering the office with glass shards. As Brad had anticipated, bullets whined hither and thither like a swarm of angry bees. As he suspected, the chances of being hit by ricochet were unpleasantly high.

"That's just for starters!" Holliger shouted. "Now see sense and come on out."

Ewen pulled a weapon free clear of the securing chain. To his disgust Brad saw it was an example of the vintage cap-lock Colt shot-gun of the type he'd been issued with in the war. A more useless weapon he couldn't have conceived of . . .

"Come on, you got no time left, Ranger!" Morgan Holliger shouted.

"This gun is absolutely bloody useless," Lord Ewen murmured. "I really do believe that at this juncture, discretion would be the better part of valour, don't you, old chap?"

Brad stared at him, open-mouthed.

"That is to say, I think a little negotiation mightn't come amiss," Lord Ewen explained apologetically. "You know, trade the prisoner in and live to fight another day, what? After all, we aren't dealing with savages."

"I wouldn't count on that," Brad said.

At that moment another volley of shots poured through the gaping window. Both men ducked as some hit the bars of the cell with a shower of sparks evoking a shout of fear from the occupant.

"Look, Sergeant Saunders, I really must insist that we negotiate . . . "

"Negotiate with Holliger?" Brad said incredulously. "You gotta be joking! You ain't in the British Army now. They ain't gonna let us walk out with flags flying and a band playin'. Those days are long gone."

"I thought you might say that," Ewen murmured.

As Brad turned away to watch the window, Lord Ewen reversed the shot-gun he was holding and swung it.

From the cell, Lee Holliger watched open-mouthed as the butt cracked against Brad's skull and he slumped forward on to the floor limp as a rag doll.

"I really am fearfully sorry about that old chap," Lord Ewen said as he tossed his weapon away. "But I couldn't wait any longer for you to decide to play the hero, I'm afraid."

He bent down and with a show of strength which belied his slim stature, he hoisted Brad on to his shoulder.

"Hey, what about me?" Lee Holliger shouted.

The sparks had ignited some posters on a notice board close to the window. The flames had caught hold and were crackling fiercely. One blazing poster floated away from the wall. Before Lee Holliger's terrified gaze, the paper landed on the sheriff's desk and the tiny flames began to lick at a pile of papers.

"Christ! We're gonna fry in here!" Lee Holliger exclaimed.

Lord Ewen picked up the keys from the desk and handed them to Holliger as he headed for the door at the back.

"My dear boy," he said. "Don't panic, all is not lost. One of these keys should fit the lock. Do see yourself out, won't you."

Lord Ewen ignored the explosion of oaths as Lee snatched the keys off him. He opened the door at the rear of the premises and slipped out into an alley.

After the flames in the office, the night sky was as black as pitch. A cat brushed Ewen's legs as it darted past him. He followed it, bracing himself under the ranger's weight. He had made almost the full length of the alley before he stumbled against a metal trash can, the lid of which dropped off and rolled around in ever-decreasing circles until it fell with a clatter.

"There he goes!" a voice shouted from behind.

Bending low, Lord Ewen continued the last few yards pursued by a hail of bullets.

Rounding a corner, he paused, gasping for breath. He was out into one of the streets now. Pools of yellow light illuminated the boardwalks. The pounding of feet behind him roused him to make a further seemingly futile effort to put ground between himself and his pursuers.

At that moment a man on horseback appeared in the street ahead of him. Beyond him he could see shadowy figures running hither and thither. The rider spotted Lord Ewen immediately and spurred his mount towards him, brandishing a hand-gun.

"A horse!" Lord Ewen quoted to himself. "My kingdom for a horse!"

"Stay right there, Mr Sheepherder, I guess that's as far as you're goin'," the rider shouted.

"Good evening," Lord Ewen said pleasantly. "I wonder if I might prevail on you to assist me?"

As he spoke, he dropped Brad about as gently as he would a sack of potatoes.

The rider dismounted and, holding his horse with one hand and the weapon in the other, advanced towards him. At the same moment a crowd of pursuers emerged from the alley.

"OK, boys, I got him!" the dismounted rider called out.

His words died on his lips as Lord Ewen delivered a straight left which impacted full on his jaw, snapping his head back with numbing force. As he slumped to the ground, out cold, Lord Ewen bent down, snatched up his gun and scattered the men from the alley with a volley of randomly aimed shots.

He picked Brad up and in one easy movement laid him across the saddle of the horse. As he leapt into the saddle and spurred the animal into flight, the guns behind erupted into a spattering of ill-aimed shots which only served to make his mount go faster.

Once clear of the town, Lord Ewen reined in, listening for sounds of pursuit, but there were none. In front of him lay the flickering fires of the circus encampment. Deciding it was useless to keep on riding blindly into the night, he resolved to seek refuge there. If the circus people were hostile, then he'd have to think of somewhere else.

As he turned in at the box-office he found his way blocked by the enormous bulk of a woman.

"Good evening, madam, please allow me to introduce myself. My name is Charles Ewen — er Lord Charles Ewen, actually. I should esteem it if you would do me a small favour."

"What the hell do you want, mister?" Dolly Bailey demanded, hands on hips. "The show don't open 'til tomorrow and the way this town's shapin' you won't need to book in advance." She peered curiously into the darkness. "Say, who've you got there?"

"Madam, I have here with me a gentleman who has had the misfortune to take a nasty crack on the head," Lord Ewen replied. "I would take him back home with me, but I fear the journey will be too long and uncomfortable for him."

Mystified, Dolly walked across to Ewen's horse. She stared at the inert body draped over the saddle.

"Why you got Ranger Saunders here!" she exclaimed.

"Oh, so you've been introduced? I say, that is a relief! I really don't like to impose on you like this," Ewen replied.

Dolly's eyes narrowed. "I guess you must be that sheepman who's causing all the trouble round here?"

"For my sins, madam, I believe that is the case."

"Mister, do you always use ten words when one would do?"

Before he could reply. Dolly lifted Brad off the horse and laid him down close to the fire. As she tossed a blanket over him, he gave a groan.

Dolly sighed. "Well, I guess it looks like we're all in trouble."

"Then, please may I leave him with you, madam?" Lord Ewen enquired.

"OK, but you'd better get the hell outa here, Mister Lord Ewen. I got me enough trouble with this ranger-boy to look after without you hangin' around as well."

* * *

By the time Lee Holliger had opened the lock to his cell and made his break for freedom, the fire in the sheriff's office was uncomfortably ablaze.

"What the hell were you playing at?" Lee demanded as his brother appeared in the doorway. "I could've fried in there."

"Well, we got a fire engine so you didn't, did you?" Morgan replied callously. He listened with incredulity when Lee explained what had happened.

"Are you seriously tellin' me that Ewen slugged the ranger an' made off with him?" he demanded.

When Lee nodded, Morgan went on, "Well, they can't have got far, that's for sure." He glanced round him, the masks had disappeared and the men had joined in with the townsfolk to

126

watch the fire engine and its team at work.

At that moment, a man appeared at a run, breathless.

"Say, boss, we just seen Ewen ride off with the ranger."

"Well, don't just stand there, get after him, then!" Morgan shouted. "Lee, go over to the saloon, grab some of the boys and start lookin' for 'em. They can't get far at night. Whatever you do, make sure you find 'em."

"What are you gonna do?" Lee demanded.

"Me? I'm goin' back to that poker game. The situation there is kinda crucial."

"But what do I do if I find 'em?" Lee called after his brother.

"What you were gonna do anyway back at the saloon," came the terse reply. "Only don't mess it up this time."

★ ★ ★

As the first golden rays of dawn blazed over the low hills surrounding Chanceville, Willi von Faulkenburg raised his bleary eyes to meet those of his adversary across the poker table in the Graveyard Saloon.

No emotion showed in Morgan Holliger's face, despite the five hours he had been playing, as Willi slid the remainder of his chips forward in a call to equalize the betting interval which involved only the two of them.

"Showdown," muttered Carter Rankin.

Jackson Venn started out of his doze. Lance Quirk and Hank Weaver yawned simultaneously. Frank Brock drew heavily on his cigar and leaned forward.

Willi was a fraction first to lay down his cards. Not a word was spoken as the eyes of the onlookers read four of a kind.

The tension rose as Morgan laid his cards in front of him.

"My God, it's a straight flush," Venn

said on the end of a sharp intake of breath.

Brock gave a low whistle.

"Willi, you just lost fifty thousand dollars," he said in a voice as hushed as if he were speaking in a cathedral.

Willi buried his face in his hands, the only sign of emotion he had shown all night.

"I'll take your IOU for now," Morgan said with a smug smile. "We can settle up later."

All the men knew exactly what that meant — the fate of the Iron Cross ranch had been decided.

"You took a hell of a risk, but I think you can rip that letter up," Frank Brock murmured to Holliger as both men rose to their feet.

"I wonder if Lee's had any luck finding Ewen?" Venn remarked as the school broke up. "I reckon it's time we got this sheepherdin' business finished once and for all."

Willi didn't hear the reply as he headed for the door. Outside the gambling suite, the smell of perfume overpowered the stale sweat and cigar smoke which had pervaded the atmosphere.

As he left the room a slim hand gripped his arm.

"Not now, Alabama," he muttered.

"Right now," she insisted.

And Willi didn't feel disposed to argue.

★ ★ ★

"Well now, you finally got him in bed — an' he ain't much use to you," Dolly Bailey murmured ironically as she gazed at the inert figure of the ranger.

Brad's eyes flicked open and he winced as she touched the egg-shaped lump an the side of his head.

"What happened?" Brad demanded.

His vision cleared dramatically at the sight of Dolly's magnificent cleavage as she leant over him.

"Looks like you got yourself into a

fight," she told him. "An Englishman rescued you and brought you here outa harm's way."

"Lord Ewen?"

"Yep, that's the one. Talks like he's got a mouth permanently full of blueberry pie. He ain't here now, though."

"I'd best get goin'."

As Brad made to get up, Dolly pushed him back down again.

"You're not fit to get up yet," she told him. "You rest some more."

"I can't lie here," Brad protested. "I got things to do."

"OK," Dolly said resignedly. "But I guess you ain't goin' no place without breakfast."

There was a noise outside and Dolly moved to open the wagon flap. Outside she saw one of the hands.

"Say, ma'am, there's a bunch of guys out here lookin' fer somebody. They say they're gonna search the camp," he said.

"They're what?" Dolly roared.

The wagon-bed rocked as Dolly eased her bulk down the steps and went outside. Inside, Brad eased himself on to his elbow and reached for his gunbelt.

But he had no need of it, for through a chink in the canvas he witnessed one of the most remarkable routs of all time. Dolly Bailey, hands on hips, temper roused, was a truly formidable sight.

"You guys wanna search my camp?" she roared at Lee Holliger and his *compadres*. "OK, big boys, you can make a start right over there in the lions' cage. An' don't blame me if them big cats don't like it. They ain't been fed yet."

* * *

The morning was well-advanced when a buggy drew up outside the sheriff's office in Chanceville.

Augusta stepped down and stared at the fire-damaged building.

"Mornin' Miss von Faulkenburg. I am afraid the sheriff is otherwise engaged. Can I assist you in any way? May I take you for coffee?"

She turned to face Frank Brock who was approaching along the boardwalk. Snappily dressed in a medium grey suit the banker was carrying a silver-topped walking cane. The only sign of the loss of the previous night's sleep was a slight bagginess under his eyes.

"I really must speak with my brother, Mr Brock. It's urgent. Have you any idea where I might find him?"

The banker had the grace to blanch under his tan. Clearly Augusta did not know what had happened last night. "Well, now, see here, ma'am, I guess he's . . . "

"Where? Not still over at the saloon, surely, not at this hour of the morning."

Augusta picked up her skirts and swept off in the direction of the Graveyard Saloon. Frank Brock hastened after her.

"Now listen Miss von Faulkenburg.

This place ain't the kinda place a good woman should be seen in — if you follow me."

Augusta paused underneath the sign aware of the open-mouthed gaze of two cowhands lounging on the boardwalk.

"I think I follow you very well, Mr Brock. If this is where he is, perhaps you will kindly go inside and ask him to come out here and talk with me."

Hearing the sound of voices brought Carter Rankin to the batwings.

"Hell's teeth, has she heard what's happened already?" the saloon owner muttered in reply to Frank Brock's request.

"I don't think so — but it ain't gonna be me who tells her, that's for sure," Brock replied. "Now fetch that boy out here sharp before she asks any more embarrassin' questions."

When the banker rejoined her, Augusta said, "Mr Brock, just what has been happening here in Chanceville?"

She listened in silence as he told her of Lord Ewen's confrontation with

Lee Holliger and the subsequent events at the sheriff's office. However, he contrived very neatly to avoid any mention of the disastrous consequences of the poker game.

"So it seems that Morgan Holliger has declared war on the law," she said grimly when Brock had finished.

"I guess so," Brock replied sombrely. "I sure hope that man knows what he's doin'."

"Couldn't any of you stop him?" Augusta demanded. When Brock made no answer she gave him a contemptuous look. "You are frightened of him, perhaps? And no doubt it is convenient for you to hide behind him."

Brock stiffened. "Your father would never have spoken to me like that," he said.

"Do not presume to put words in my father's mouth," Augusta flashed back. "He was more of a man than any of you."

His words reminded Augusta of her doleful errand and she was just about to tell Brock, when Willi appeared. His handsome face showed signs of the ravages of the previous night's debauchery.

"Well now, I guess I'll be gettin' along, Miss von Faulkenburg," Brock said, raising his stetson.

"Thank you, Mr Brock, I'm obliged to you," Augusta said. She rounded on her brother. "And now, Wilhelm," she said, speaking in German. "Will you please take me somewhere respectable, for I have something to tell you."

"Has father died?" Willi asked her as they crossed the street and entered Weaver's Hotel. The lobby clerk hurriedly showed them through to the restaurant where Willi ordered coffee.

"Well?" he enquired.

"Yes, he died early yesterday evening."

"I am sorry." Willi mouthed the words making no effort to hide his elation.

"Oh come on, Willi, you can't mean that. He was asking for you. You knew how ill he was. I sent a message for you to come and see him, but you didn't come," Augusta said stonily.

Willi waited until the waitress had poured the coffee and left them alone before he patted Augusta's hand.

"I am sorry, I truly am," Willi said. "I was intending to visit him. But I had some urgent business here in town. I really had no idea he was so close to death."

There was contempt in Augusta's eyes as they met his. "I don't believe you, Willi," she said. "I made his condition perfectly clear. You didn't come to see him because you knew you would have to tell him what a mess you have made of your life."

"Augusta, that's not fair . . . "

"It isn't, I know, but it happens to be true. And now something bad has happened here, I know it."

A crafty look appeared in Willi's eyes.

"When is the funeral?" he enquired.

"It will be the day after tomorrow. Papa wanted to be buried on the ranch.

He told me the exact spot."

Willi frowned. "It isn't very convenient. I should have thought the town cemetery would have been more suitable."

"It was his last wish," Augusta insisted. "And I insist that we respect it. Your convenience is my last concern."

"Oh very well, let me know when it is and I'll be there," Willi promised.

"To hear the Will being read, no doubt."

"But of course," he replied with a sly smile.

Augusta finished her coffee and rose to her feet.

"Very well, I will go and inform Mr Tuttle. After that, I'm going back to the ranch. You can find out the funeral arrangements from him later today."

8

"NOW just what do you think you're doin'?" Dolly demanded.

She trickled her finger down Brad's slab-muscled chest with undisguised admiration in her eyes as he slipped on his flannel shirt.

"Why, I guess I got things to do," he replied as he stooped to pull on his pants.

"But you ain't in no fit condition," Dolly said heatedly.

"I'll live," Brad said as he put on his vest.

"Now you listen to me, boy. I've seen more knocks runnin' this outfit than you ever dreamed about. What I always tell 'em is you gotta take care of yourself if you wanna play another show."

"Sure, Dolly," Brad replied as he strapped on his gunbelt.

With all his clothes on, he felt safe at last. He fingered the lump on the back of his head gingerly. Maybe Dolly was right. His head still felt as though someone was pounding rocks inside it.

"How the hell did I come by this?"

The circus-owner's ample shoulders heaved in a shrug. "I dunno. But that English lord said you'd done taken a nasty crack on the head. Now how did you come by that, I wonder?"

Brad nodded. Someday that was a question he'd like to hear an answer to.

"Lord Ewen? Where is he now?"

"He said he was headin' back to his ranch. Best place for him, I guess. This whole town's bayin' after his blood. What in the world made him bring sheep right into the heart of Texas? It's like lettin' a herd of antelope loose near my lions' cage with the door wide open."

Brad nodded. Despite his opinion about what Ewen was doing, his respect for the Englishman had gone up a notch, for somehow he had rescued him from an impossible situation back there in Grant's office. That wasn't the action of a guy who didn't know what he was about.

What to do?

He figured his best plan was to get out there, keep out of sight, look around, wait and watch, keep 'em guessing, play the will o' the wisp and then pounce when the moment was opportune. As McNelly had once remarked in one of his more conversational moments, "Only take out the ringleaders, boys, and the rest of the rabble will just fade away . . ."

It was a sentiment with which Brad was well suited.

"Dolly, I gotta ask a favour of you," he said.

The circus boss tossed her head. "Why, Brad, I thought you'd never ask," she said archly. "You wanna start with a kiss, maybe?"

He grinned. That Dolly had struck a

light for him was plain to see. "Look I ain't got time. Right now I need to get into town and recover my horse."

"Without bein' seen?" She heaved a sigh. "OK, if you insist, that's easy enough, I reckon. I'll take you in the buckboard. The first show is this afternoon. I wanna check if my bills have been posted. But before we go, you and me are gonna eat."

Twenty minutes later after a massive breakfast of steak and eggs, washed with coffee, Brad found himself trying to hold it down, lying under an evil-smelling tarpaulin that had been used to cover God-knows-what inside the well of a buckboard Dolly herself was driving into Chanceville.

The journey was hot and bumpy, and did nothing to relieve the pounding in his head, but it was mercifully short.

"Take care of my hoss, mister, while I do some shoppin'," Brad heard Dolly say to the man in charge at the livery.

"Don't spend it all at once, ma'am,"

the man remarked good-humouredly.

"It won't have come from any pockets hereabouts, that's fer sure. I sure don't know why I bothered pitching my big top at this town. Bookin's are right down. I gotta funny feelin' no one's interested in seein' a circus right now. Say what gives? Everyone's as jumpy as a steer on a moonlit night," Dolly remarked.

"It's like you surmise, ma'am. The whole town's sky-high," the man replied.

"So what's the cause?"

"Why a ranger rode in and sided with a lousy sheepherdin' Englishman, name of Lord Ewen. Morgan Holliger, one of the biggest cattlemen hereabouts, ordered his boys to run 'em outa town. Good luck to 'em, I say. It's high time somebody did something. We don't want nobody tellin' us what we can and can't do — 'specially when it's an English lord raising sheep. Say, ma'am, how about we round up a few fer your lions to eat? It'll save you a few dollars. Say, I've heard a lot about you. How's about I call round your place? You could cook me a mutton chop."

"Pigs might fly an' monkeys chew tobacco," Dolly retorted. "Me, I cook breakfast fer real men, not horse-shit shovellers."

"Phew, now there goes one hell of a woman," the man exclaimed as the stable door banged shut behind the retreating Dolly.

Brad turned back one corner of the tarpaulin and slipped down from the buckboard. The livery man had his back turned. Whistling softly to himself, he was not aware of Brad's stealthy approach until he felt the cold muzzle of a Peacemaker jab into his neck.

"What the hell's goin' on?" he ejaculated.

"Take it easy. I could've sent you to sleep with the butt," Brad told him. "But I didn't want for you not to know I just stopped by for my hoss."

"Best thing fer you to do, Ranger,

is get outa town as fast as you can," the man said sullenly when he had recovered his equilibrium.

"I figured that," Brad agreed. "Just remember you never saw me."

Which was the opposite of what he intended . . .

★ ★ ★

"I swear I had him cold, but I'm tellin' you iffen I'd stuck around I'd have been blown apart. Why this other guy was firing *artillery* at me."

Holliger had just completed giving the Iron Cross foreman an account of his unsuccessful attempt to bushwhack Brad. He eased his horse clear of a thicket of shinnery oak and peered at the Iron Cross ranch house silhouetted on the skyline.

"Who was this other guy d'you reckon?" Pate queried.

Holliger thought for a moment. Suddenly he snapped his fingers. "Say, wait a minute. I noticed one of Ewen's herder's on the skyline as I rode along the trail."

Pate nodded. "I bet it was him. Word is those guys are arming themselves with whatever weapons they can get."

"If they want it rough, they can have it," Holliger said savagely. "Ain't no way they're gonna win. Lee's gone out with some of the boys today."

"What about the ranger?"

"I ain't gonna worry no more about him, Ezra. There's been no sign of him for the last twenty-four hours since he rode outa town. He knows he ain't wanted round here. The situation is well under control. We shan't be seeing him again, iffen he knows what's good for him."

"I wouldn't count on it," Pate said darkly. "Those guys ain't noted for giving up easy. Recollect he's got McNelly to report back to — and that guy don't take no for an answer, that's fer sure."

Holliger laughed. "McNelly won't trouble us no more. Didn't you know he'd died? Some greenhorn called Hall has taken over. By the time that ranger has reported back to him, we'll have Ewen off this range and not a sheep in sight. D'you reckon Sergeant Saunders will dare to tell his new captain exactly how it happened here?"

Pate nodded. "OK, I'll buy that. But don't forget I still got three hundred steers to rebrand and shift up the line. If anyone finds 'em, that's us finished for sure."

Holliger fished out a muslin sack of Ridgewood Tobacco and rolled a smoke.

"Don't worry, Ezra. The ranger's gone. Lee and the boys are gonna keep on harassing Ewen's sheepherders. They'll be too busy taking care of their own skins to go sniffin' round where they're not wanted. By the way, what's happening with that herder the ranger brought here?"

"Doc Kearnsey called this morning. He certified the baron's death and took a look at the herder. He's gonna survive. Miss von Faulkenburg sent one of the boys over to tell Lord Ewen. He sent word back to say he'll come over and pick him up tomorrow."

The two men's eyes met with the look of conspirators.

"Be nice if neither of them never made the journey back," Holliger remarked.

"Funny, I was thinking the same way," Pate replied. "It just could be that he came about some kinda mishap."

"OK. I'll put Lee and the boys on to it." Holliger drew in a lungful of smoke. "By the way, you know now the baron's dead, Willi is set to inherit the Iron Cross?"

Pate nodded.

"Well, not for long I guess. I reckon you'll find that he's said goodbye to his inheritance before he's even said hello."

Pate stared at Holliger who laughed harshly.

"Ezra, I guess it's time you knew that

148

last night Willi gambled the Iron Cross and lost."

"To you?"

Holliger nodded. "First time I set eyes on him I had him for a tinhorn. I've been setting him up for this."

"Jesus Christ! Well, I guess it ain't the first time a ranch has been lost on the turn of a card. I take it Miss von Faulkenburg doesn't know yet?"

"No — and I'd be obliged if you'd keep it to yourself until after the Will is read."

"There's no chance of that. As far as she's concerned I'm on the same level as cow-dirt. Wouldn't I like to see the look on her face when she finds out — by the way, I take it you ain't still aspirin' to marry her?"

"Marry her?" Holliger guffawed. "Me, marry that horse-faced bitch! Nothing is gonna please me more than to see her crawl."

"If you take over the Iron Cross, I take it you'll still be needin' a foreman?"

"Sure, Ezra. You stick around. After we've gotten rid of Lord Ewen, between us we're gonna turn these two ranches and that little operation of yours into something big."

* * *

Brad led Blaze out of the livery stable the way any cowboy would, mounted and rode off in a canter. By behaving normally, he excited no one's attention in the busy street and within minutes he had cleared the town confident that no one except the livery man had seen him.

His first concern was to find the location of Ewen's ranch so he left the trail which led to the Iron Cross and followed a parallel route skirting past a couple of small outfits, either the owners of which or their wives could have directed him but he did not do that, preferring to push on in the general direction of the site where he had discovered Lord Ewen's slaughtered flock.

As he rode, his eyes swept the country constantly, making mental note of landmarks, so that he could orientate himself readily should the need arise.

By noon he had cut across a trail he reckoned ran in one direction towards the Iron Cross. From the increasing frequency of odd strands of wool caught on low bushes, he figured the other way must lead in the direction of Ewen's place.

Turning towards the latter, he left the trail and headed along the bank of a broad stream across open, rolling country covered with grass and stands of shinnery oak leading in the direction of some low hills. Once on the higher ground, he would be able to use his spy-glass to better effect.

His judgement was vindicated for the further he rode, the more he came across small groups of grazing sheep which had been recently shorn.

By evening he had reached one of the hills. He dismounted and after tethering Blaze made camp beside the higher reaches of the stream. Tiredness took over and after a frugal meal of beans and bacon washed down with coffee, he wrapped himself in his blanket and spent the night under the stars.

The following morning, he continued his survey of the open range. There were cattle everywhere, carrying principally the Iron Cross and Lazy Y brands along with a sprinkling of one or two others. Interspersed with them, sheep were scattered all over the place hidden in gullies and draws, peeping out at him from patches of scrub oak. It was plain that Lord Ewen was running quite a large-scale operation and, from the way the sheep had spread out over the range, it was easy to see why the cattlemen were so angry.

So far the vast landscape had been devoid of any sign of man but as noon approached, Brad spotted three riders moving on the horizon. Taking out his brass-bound spy-glass he focussed it and instantly identified one of them as Ezra Pate, the Iron Cross foreman.

Taking the greatest of care to avoid detection, Brad followed them until it was apparent that they were heading towards a cabin in a small secluded valley in a remote part of the hills many miles away from the Iron Cross ranch house.

Here there were no more sheep, but from a rocky eminence, Brad observed a herd of around 300 head of cattle grazing peacefully on the lush grass in the vicinity of the cabin. The ranch foreman stopped halfway down into the valley, his men flanking him on either side. To all intents he was checking out part of the Iron Cross herd — which was no more than his job.

Brad waited patiently until Pate and his men spurred their horses down the slope to the valley bottom and dismounted at the cabin. From his vantage point Brad saw one of the men preparing and light a fire. Pate emerged from the cabin and thrust an iron bar into the embers. The two cowboys mounted their horses and circled the herd. In a matter of minutes, they had cut out a steer, and driven it back to the cabin.

The two hands roped the steer and brought it down close by the fire. The animal's bawling echoed in the low hills as Pate applied the branding iron.

After a couple of hours of work, the men brewed java and then made their way out of the valley.

Once they had gone, curiosity compelled Brad to ride down into the valley. The cabin yielded signs of regular use. Inside there were a couple of blankets, some cooking utensils and there was an ample supply of canned food in a cupboard. Brad thought little of it as he set about making himself a brew on the dying embers of the fire. Plenty of ranching operations maintained such places as this for use in winter as line cabins.

But as he sipped his drink he noticed the branding iron lying on the floor.

It was still radiating heat as he looked at it, expecting to see the Iron Cross brand, but instead there was a little curl at the tip.

Brad had been born and raised with cattle in the Panhandle. After the war he had worked as a stock detective. There was nothing he did not know about cattle, legal or illegal. The significance of this seemingly innocuous piece of iron was not lost on him. He knew he was holding the hallmark of a rustler — a running iron, the tool with which in the hands of an expert brands could be altered beyond recognition.

Brad went outside, mounted Blaze and took a look round the grazing herd. By riding softly he was able to get in close enough to read the brands. They weren't the Iron Cross, that was for sure. Some were half-diamond and some were full-diamond — brands he hadn't seen anywhere in this area.

There was no doubt in his mind as to what was going on. Clearly Ezra Pate was receiving stolen cattle and altering the brands. The change from half diamond to full-diamond was a relatively simple one for an artist with a running iron to make.

Brad dismounted and rolled a smoke. The more he thought about it, the more it made sense. From what he'd learned from Augusta von Faulkenburg, Ezra Pate worked for a man who didn't regard it his business to patrol the range, checking out on his foreman. It would be easy for Pate to move small consignments of rustled cattle across the open range and hold them in the remote valley whilst he changed the brands at leisure. Once that was done, they could be passed further along the chain and any chance of linking them to him would be lost forever.

It also explained the hostility Pate had shown towards the sheepherder. With Ewen's men roaming the area with flocks of sheep, the chances of his operation being discovered must have increased uncomfortably.

By late afternoon Brad was standing

on a bluff with a sheer drop of around 300 feet looking down on the trail winding across the rolling countryside. On the horizon, he thought he saw a trace of smoke. His spy-glass, when brought into focus, revealed the presence of a dwelling — Lord Ewen's ranch, he surmised.

He snapped the instrument shut and made his way back down to where he had left Blaze. Parched and hungry after the day's work, he decided it was time to satisfy both needs. But as he set about gathering some twigs for a fire, the noise of gunfire attracted his attention.

Throwing down his armful of kindling, he raced with giant strides over to Blaze, snatched his Winchester out of its scabbard and raced back up the hill.

From the bluff, he saw a single covered wagon being driven hell-for-leather along the trail. Through the cloud of dust rising behind it Brad caught sight of orange flashes followed by the reports from the muzzles of the guns of half-a-dozen pursuers who came boiling over a rim in the land. Brad waited as the wagon came closer. It was clear the driver had no chance of eluding his pursuers — and the riders were drawing closer and closer . . .

He laid aside the spy-glass, took up his Winchester and, lying on his belly, took aim. He estimated that the range was never going to be closer than a thousand yards. At that range, accurate shooting was impossible, so Brad opted for a rapid rate of fire in the hope of driving off the attackers.

The leading pursuer was closing in on the wagon as Brad squeezed off the first of fifteen rapid consecutive shots into the dust cloud.

As Brad reloaded the Winchester, he saw the wagon was still maintaining its progress. As the dust cloud swirled away, he saw the pursuers had come to a stop and were bunched together, as if uncertain where the shots had come from. A riderless horse was careering loose on the range, indicating he must have got lucky with one shot.

Brad went down on one knee and took aim once more. His first shot must have been close, for the riders didn't wait for more. As he emptied the magazine, they turned in full retreat. He watched their withdrawal through his spy-glass, noting that one horse was carrying two riders.

Satisfied, Brad rose to his feet but as he turned, a slight noise made him whirl round . . . the little Mexican came closer, his long coat flapping about his ankles, his dog following obediently.

"*Buenos dias, Señor Diego Gonzales!*" he exclaimed.

The herder's leathery face creased into a smile at Brad's courtesy.

"*Buenos dias, señor.*"

"What's been going on down there?" Brad asked, continuing in Spanish.

"You were doing the same for Lord Ewen as I did for you, *señor*," Diego replied with a delighted smile. "Those men attacked him. You just saved their lives."

"Who were those men?"

"I think perhaps they are *vaqueros*," he replied guardedly.

"I reckon I'd better go see Lord Ewen," Brad said.

He returned to the bottom of the hill, finished making a fire and shared a brew of java with the Mexican herder.

"How many sheep is Lord Ewen running on this range?" Brad enquired.

"Five thousand," the herder replied.

Brad whistled. "And how many herders?"

"There are five of us. We each look after a thousand sheep."

"Did you not realize when you came to work here that there would be trouble from the cattlemen?"

The herder nodded. "When they can find us," he said with a grin. "Lord Ewen offered us ten dollars a month extra to work for him."

"An offer you couldn't refuse," Brad remarked.

"Sometimes a man has no choice."

"So you will stay?"

"But of course. A good shepherd does not desert his sheep."

Brad tossed the dregs from his mug into the fire. The religious significance of the remark was not lost on him.

"The Texans will have to kill us, we will not be driven away," the herder said. "One day they will realize that they are wrong and men will raise cattle and sheep together in peace."

Brad saddled Blaze. After he had mounted, he turned to say farewell but the herder and his dog had vanished into the wilderness.

Brad rode away from the hills, following a line across country running parallel to the trail which led to Ewen's ranch. He intercepted the trail about a mile before his destination and approached the ranch openly.

Shearing was in progress as Brad walked Blaze into the yard past a large wagon packed with fleeces. As he paused to watch the shearer work his hand-clippers, he had to admire the skill and dexterity with which he removed the fleece.

"How do you do, Sergeant Saunders?" Lord Ewen stepped down off the stoop to greet him. Behind him Brad caught the glint of sunshine on the blade of a meat cleaver in the hand of a Chinaman hovering in the background.

"Howdy," Brad replied. "I guess I just repaid me a debt I owed you just now."

"Really?" Lord Ewen's face remained expressionless as he produced a packet of cheroots and shared them with Brad. "I suspected it might be you who fired at those men, although I had heard you'd left the county."

"Is Carlos OK?"

Ewen nodded. "Thanks to you, again."

"I still can't figure out how I came by this. No bullet did it, that's fer sure," Brad said, as he fingered the bump on the back of his head. He eyed Lord Ewen with open suspicion.

"Dolly Bailey reckoned it was you who brought me to her place."

Lord Ewen nodded. "I could hardly leave an injured man to that pack of wolves, could I? The tender mercies of Dolly were infinitely more agreeable, I should imagine."

Brad accepted his joshing with a wry smile. Although they were worlds apart, he was rapidly developing a healthy respect for this elegant Englishman.

"Well thanks, anyway," he said.

The two men's hands met in a firm clasp.

"Looks like the cattlemen ain't gonna leave you be," Brad reflected. "By the way, how is the baron?"

"He has died, I'm afraid."

"I'm sorry to hear that. When is the funeral?"

"Tomorrow. After the doctor called, Augusta . . . er Miss von Faulkenburg, rode into town to tell her brother and make the funeral arrangements. The burial is to be at the ranch — her father wanted to be buried on his own land." Lord Ewen hesitated. "Are you aware of the situation regarding Miss von Faulkenburg's brother, Sergeant Saunders?"

Brad nodded. "She told me she thought he would inherit the ranch."

"Well, we'll just have to wait and see when the Will is read," Lord Ewen said thoughtfully.

"I take it you won't be goin' to the funeral?"

Lord Ewen blew a smoke ring and smiled.

"I wouldn't advise it," Brad warned. "You've got too many enemies, you must know that."

"You just try and keep me away," Lord Ewen said.

9

AFTER he had left Brad, Diego went back to his task of rounding up the remaining sheep which needed shearing. He'd been gathering these in small numbers all day, herding them with the aid of his dog into a pen he had built at the foot of the low hills about five miles away from the ranch.

What puzzled Diego was why the men who had attacked the wagon had withdrawn completely. Surely natural curiosity would compel them to try to find out who had attacked them?

Although the late-afternoon sun was hot, Diego set about completing his day's work with meticulous attention. Riding his burro, and using his dog, he patiently combed the remote gullies, flushing out the sheep grazing in the deep shade in twos and threes, driving them back to the pen which he had carefully sited near the higher reaches of Pilson's Creek close to some tall trees to provide the animals with water and relief from the heat of the sun. During the course of the day, he had covered several square miles of ground and had some 300 sheep safely ensconced inside the pen. After a frugal meal of beans, some coffee and an hour's rest, he would drive them to the ranch ready for shearing early next day.

As Diego went to open the pen, the sound of a snorting horse attracted his attention. Perhaps that was Lord Ewen, the *major-domo* as he would have been called on a Mexican sheep ranch, come to see how he was getting on.

As he looked round, the gentle smile which graced his wrinkled face disappeared. He stared at the group of half-a-dozen masked riders who surrounded him with mounting apprehension.

"*Dios mio!*" Diego exclaimed fervently.

"You were told to get outa this area,"

the man leading the riders rapped.

"He doesn't understand the lingo," another said contemptuously as Diego shrugged his shoulders.

"OK, boys, then let's teach this greaser a lesson he ain't gonna forget," the first man said.

There was a creak of leather as one of the riders dismounted and opened the pen. When Diego's dog rushed forward, barking furiously, the leader upholstered his revolver and killed it.

Before Diego could react, the sound of the shot stampeded the already nervous sheep and they came pouring out of the pen.

"Whoa there!" the leader shouted. "Come on, round 'em up, boys!"

The riders, although caught completely by surprise, reacted swiftly. Whooping and yelling, they chased after the sheep, heading them off and trying to force the terrified animals into a compact bunch.

Rounding up sheep was a different proposition to cattle and the riders floundered around yelling and shouting, which all added to the confusion. It was plain that in their efforts to control the sheep, Diego had been completely forgotten.

The round-up eventually succeeded but Diego stood watching, puzzled. Why were they now driving them uphill?

Suddenly the riders' ultimate intention dawned on him. He ran across to his burro and retrieved his ancient flintlock from its scabbard. He wasted precious seconds loading it, before he set off up the hill, leaping nimbly from rock to rock, taking the shortest possible route to the top by which he hoped to intercept the arrival of the masked men driving the fear-crazed flock.

Diego arrived at the top of the hill in time to witness the inevitable outcome of the stampede towards the bluff. Numb with apprehension he could do nothing except watch. The masked riders had learned quickly, for they now had the sheep in a compact mass and were driving them forward relentlessly.

Powerless to do anything to prevent it, Diego was forced to witness the wanton destruction of his flock as they poured over the sheer drop on to the jagged rocks below. It was all over in seconds. The air was full of falling sheep and the masked riders, gathered in a silent bunch along the edge of the bluff, stood as if in awe of what they had just accomplished.

In their preoccupation, they were totally unaware of Diego, tears pouring down his face, crouching in the rocks barely sixty yards away from them.

Suddenly, a cold determination to exact revenge possessed the soul of Diego. With the cold, calculating precision of a hunter, he located the man in the group who was responsible for the dead — the leader who had given the orders.

To his satisfaction, he perceived that his target was within range of his ancient weapon. The steel muzzle felt ice cold to his touch as he settled himself firmly in the rocks and took aim. Last time, he had missed intentionally, for it had never been in his mind to kill the man who had stalked the Texas Ranger.

But this time he would not miss.

The men were still bunched in a tight group, at the edge of the bluff, peering over the edge, inspecting the result of their macabre deed. They were laughing and talking animatedly in the way of men who have just achieved something, be it right or wrong.

Diego, lying in the rocks, as much part of the drab heat-seared landscape as the rocks and scrub oak, tracked the group with his gun, waiting patiently for a clear sight of the man he hated more than anyone else on earth.

The riders fanned out further apart to look over the edge. Diego's target came clearly into view. One man, and one only he could kill with his single musket ball.

His finger curled round the trigger and squeezed it . . .

The report from the musket echoed with the loudness of a small cannon off the rocks of the bluff.

In the eerie silence which followed, the smell of powder was acrid in his nostrils and Diego raised himself on to his elbows to see the effect of his shot. At first he thought he had missed, but then he saw that the rider was slumped forward in his saddle as limply as a rag doll.

As the full implication of what he had done came over him, great dread rose inside Diego — but not for retribution from the men in front of him.

"May God forgive me," he muttered, making the sign of the Cross as he scrambled to his feet.

Despite his innate fleetness of foot, Diego had no chance of escaping the wrath of the angry riders who hunted him down like a dog. No matter which escape route he sought from the barren rocks, he found it was blocked by a man holding a rifle. Bullets whined and chips of splintered rock flew about him as he stumbled this way and that.

At first, he managed to escape capture, but Diego was not a young man and his energy after his day's toil in the sun was not boundless. It was plain that the men were not shooting to kill him, for they had plenty of opportunity. Clearly, their orders were to capture him alive.

After nearly an hour of successfully evading his pursuers, they cornered him in a gully. Diego, who had long since cast his musket aside, turned to face his enemies with quiet dignity. One of them lassoed him as he would a steer and then dragged him mercilessly along the rough rocky ground back to the mouth of the gully.

Before many more minutes had elapsed, they were all there, including one man with a bloodstained bandanna tied round his head. This must be the man he thought he had killed. A surge of relief ran through Diego, his prayers had been answered. Whatever happened to him now, he was not guilty of killing a man.

"You took your time, boys," the man said angrily. He looked down at the dazed and bleeding Diego as he would a roped and helpless steer. "I guess it's high time we showed Lord Ewen that we mean business."

★ ★ ★

"By the way, I didn't get the chance to tell you that one of your herders saved my life when I was riding into Chanceville the other day," Brad said to Lord Ewen.

The Englishman listened in silence as Brad recounted the episode.

"That would be Diego," Lord Ewen said.

"Yes, that was his name. Now I'm of the opinion that Morgan Holliger is the man behind all this," Brad concluded. "D'you agree?"

Ewen nodded. "He's the hothead. The other cattlemen are quite prepared to let him shoot their bullets for them."

"That's always the way of it," Brad said. "I figured at the time that Diego knew who it was who tried to bushwhack me. But nothing would persuade him to testify, I reckon, even if I could prove it was Holliger."

"Which is hardly surprising," Lord Ewen remarked. "Diego is not stupid. He knows no jury in Texas would convict a cattleman on the word of a sheepherder."

"What I can't figure out, is how the guy got on to me," Brad said. "The only person who knew I was a ranger at that stage was Miss von Faulkenburg."

"Augusta would have nothing to do with it," Lord Ewen said curtly.

"How can you be so sure?"

Ewen shrugged.

"A hunch, perhaps?"

Ewen shook his head. "Augusta is not the kind of woman to get involved in this business. Someone must have overheard you talking to her. That foreman of hers, perhaps. He doesn't seem very trustworthy to me."

Brad nodded.

"So I take it there are no circumstances which would persuade you to leave this range?" Brad said as he prepared to leave.

"I think you know the answer to that," Lord Ewen replied quietly. "I am breaking no law, I have as much right to be here as anyone. No man has the right to use violence to make me leave. I thought this was America, the Land of the Free."

"But this is the West," Brad protested. "Anyone who ever worked with cattle hates sheep."

"For a lot of stupid, ill-conceived notions. It's an attitude that will change," Lord Ewen said. "Nothing ever stays the same. And it's so simple. Cattle like long grass, sheep prefer short. With proper land management both can co-exist and benefit from each other's presence. Men like the Baron von Faulkenburg understood this better than most. Even the most hidebound of cattleman will have to accept different ways of doing things."

"But not without a fight," Brad observed.

"Law and order will reign eventually, thanks to the efforts of men like yourself. In a hundred years time, men will look back and marvel at the things we quarrelled about. And they'll respect us, too, for the courage we showed in solving our problems."

"It's mighty fine philosophy you're makin'," Brad said. "And I agree with your sentiments. But it ain't gonna stop men like Morgan Holliger hurtin' you real bad possibly even killing you. I was born and raised the son of a cattleman up in the Panhandle. To be frank, you bein' here is making life tough for me."

"I do sympathize with your dilemma," Lord Ewen said.

"No doubt you do," Brad said. "But your sympathy don't make it any the easier, that's fer sure."

The two men's conversation was interrupted by the arrival of a herder. The young Mexican had ridden his burro hard and as he drew his animal to a halt, his terror was apparent to all the onlookers who gathered about him.

"What is it, man? What's the matter?" Lord Ewen demanded.

"Please *señor* I was driving my flock home when I saw . . . "

"Well? What did you see?"

"I was driving my flock past the bottom of the rocks when I see them."

"Saw what?"

"The others, lots of them. A whole flock. Dead. Every one of them."

Lord Ewen's face became grim. "Diego was working in that area. Did you see him?"

"No. But *señor* I am afraid. Perhaps it is well I do not go on working for you. Maybe I leave tomorrow."

"We'd best go take a look," Brad said.

"I agree," Ewen said.

He issued several curt instructions and within a few minutes a Chinaman led a fully saddled horse out of the barn.

"I take it you know where we're goin'?" Brad essayed as they left the ranch.

He wished he hadn't asked, when Ewen didn't deign to reply, merely spurring his horse into a canter towards the distant hills masked in a blue heat-haze.

An hour's hard ride, during which Brad was left in no doubt about the superb quality of the Englishman's horsemanship, brought the two men to the grisly spectacle at the foot of the bluffs.

"My God, there must be around three hundred of them," Ewen muttered as he rode round the base of the bluffs.

The buzzards which flapped among the carcasses were so gorged, they hardly moved a wing as they passed by.

"Could it have been an accident?" Brad suggested.

For the second time he winced under Ewen's scornful look.

"Sheep may be timid animals, but they aren't as stupid as cattle," he said. "I'm telling you, Sergeant Saunders, that no flock of sheep would run over the edge of a cliff unless it was driven deliberately."

"So where is Diego?" Brad said, trying to mitigate his embarrassment.

"Precisely," replied Lord Ewen.

The two men rode round the base of the hill and soon came upon the empty pen. Diego's burro scrambled to its feet as they appeared.

"Looks like they were penned up and then suddenly let go," Brad observed as he bent down to pick up a discarded fence-pole.

Ewen stayed on his horse as Brad searched the area.

"Come on, man," he said impatiently. "I want to find Diego before nightfall."

Brad straightened up. "A party of

up to a dozen men stopped by. They released the sheep from this pen and drove them up the hill and over the edge of the bluff."

"Very well," Lord Ewen said impatiently. "We have seen the result of that."

Brad stooped to pick up a rag of cloth from a bush. "Diego was here. This is from his coat. The strange thing is, he went that way." He pointed directly up the steep slope above them as he spoke.

"You mean he ran away!" Lord Ewen exclaimed.

Brad shook his head.

"Oh no, he went after them — with his musket. Look, see the scabbard on his burro is empty and here's where he spilled some powder from the horn as he loaded it."

It was Lord Ewen's turn to look at Brad with respect.

"What now?"

"We'll follow him. That is, if you're up to it."

Lord Ewen shot Brad a sideways glance before he dismounted. The two men tethered their horses and set out on foot up the steep side of the hill. Brad's keen eyes picked up the scuff marks on the rocks from the herder's boots which marked his progress.

"Well?" asked Ewen, mopping his brow as they reached the edge of the bluff. "D'you think he's down there among the sheep?"

Brad shook his head. "Diego took a shot at one of the men." He pointed to flecks of dark red on one of the rocks. "This is blood. I figure Diego wounded, maybe even killed him. Afterwards, his *compadres* spread out and hunted him down."

"So where is he now?" Ewen demanded.

"Now there we have a problem," Brad said. He straightened up and scanned the sky.

"The answer can't lie up there," Ewen said irritably.

"Not for you, maybe," Brad replied.

"But just look at yonder buzzard."

Ewen followed Brad's pointing finger until he picked up the solitary bird soaring about a mile away.

"Now why is he so far away from the rest?" Brad said. "Could it be he's found something he's keepin' to himself?"

"For once, I hope to God you're wrong," Lord Ewen replied.

The two men returned to their horses. Lord Ewen tethered the reluctant burro to his own mount and they set out in the direction which Brad had marked clearly in his mind's eye.

Dusk was gathering when Lord Ewen said, "I don't think we are going to find him. We must have searched a dozen of these gullies, now. He could be anywhere."

"Wait!" Brad leaned out of the saddle, studying the ground intently. "Someone was dragged this way. Look here are some scraps of cloth."

They pushed their horses forward into yet another gully. In the eerie half light cast by the setting sun, a corpse was swinging gently in the evening breeze. Although the eyes had already been pecked out, their ghastly bloodstained sockets seemed to be staring accusingly at them.

"Angels and Ministers of Grace defend us!" Lord Ewen exclaimed. "What manner of men did this?"

"That is what I intend to find out," Brad replied softly.

"I think your dilemma has been solved," Lord Ewen said with a shrewd glance at Brad.

10

THE noon sun shone fiercely out of a deep-blue sky laced with fleecy-white clouds, burning the bared heads of the men in the crowd of people surrounding the open grave.

Despite the short notice, the members of the Cattleman's Association and various prominent members of Chanceville's business community had suspended their animosity towards the baron and turned out in force with their wives to attend his funeral.

From a discreet distance, well hidden by a copse of shinnery oak, Brad was observing the proceedings through his spy-glass.

Augusta von Faulkenburg was at the head of the mourners, accompanied by a clergyman and a man Brad surmised was her brother, Willi. Behind them came Morgan Holliger, dressed, as were the other men and women in the party, in black.

Then came the ranch hands and servants, dressed in their Sunday-best clothes. Lord Ewen was there, too, as he had said he would be, but he was standing in the background, well away from the main party of mourners.

The formalities did not last long and then the coffin was lowered on ropes into the grave. After paying their last respects in a moment or two of silence, the mourners left the grave to be filled in by two ranch hands whilst they repaired to the house no doubt for refreshment before returning home.

Augusta, wearing a black dress with a hat and veil, waited in the deep shadow of the doorway with her brother to receive the mourners. Shaking hands with the men, she received a peck on the cheek from their wives, accepting their murmured condolences with a dignified nod.

Last of all came Lord Ewen. Dressed impeccably in a black suit, he appeared before Augusta with a polite bow.

"Please accept my sincere condolences at the death of your father," he said.

"You're taking a risk, showing your face here, aren't you?" Willi said when he realized it was Lord Ewen.

"He was our father's protégé, he has every right to be here," Augusta said stiffly.

Willi's face reddened. "Look here, Ewen, I don't see any point in you coming into the house. There are men in there who hate your guts, you must know that. I suggest that now you have paid your respects, you leave immediately."

Ewen turned to face him, his face full of contempt. "Now that your father is dead, Herr von Faulkenburg, I see you intend to side with the cattlemen, thus dishonouring all your father was trying to do."

Willi took a step forward, fists clenched. "How dare you talk to me of honour!" he shouted.

"My family's motto is 'To Serve is

to Honour'," Lord Ewen said quietly. He turned to Augusta. "Did you know that only yesterday, one of my men had his flock taken and driven over a cliff in the hills? Three hundred head of sheep fell to their deaths."

"That has nothing to do with me!" Willi's voice rose.

"We found the herder hanging from a tree."

"Is that any surprise to you?" Willi said. "Given you're not wanted round here?"

"Hold your tongue!" Augusta exclaimed. "This day of all days. Remember it is your father's funeral."

"I don't care, I want this man off my property!"

"Your property!" Augusta exclaimed. "You say this before your father is cold in his grave!"

"Your sister is right," Lord Ewen said. "In any event, it is never wise to count your chickens before they are hatched."

Beside himself, Willi flung a wild

punch at Lord Ewen. The slim Englishman parried it with ease.

"Willi, stop it!" Augusta cried as her brother charged blindly forward.

Lord Ewen side-stepped and Willi fell forward, thrashing at empty space.

"Hold it!"

Morgan Holliger emerged from the crowd of male guests who filled the corridor behind them.

"Willi's right, I reckon you'd better leave," Holliger said to Ewen. "And when you get back to your ranch, pack your bag and get out for good."

"Is that a threat?" Lord Ewen enquired calmly.

"It's not only a threat, it's a promise that if you and your sheep aren't off this range within two days, we're gonna drive you off."

"Is that you talking, or is it the Cattleman's Association?" Lord Ewen demanded. "And where is your legal authority?"

"We don't need any," Holliger said. "You just do as we say."

Hank Weaver thrust his bulk through to the front.

"It's everybody's concern, Ewen," he said harshly. "You being here is causing our town nothing but trouble. Business don't thrive on trouble. Trouble drives honest folk away. An' you're trouble, Ewen, trouble with a capital T. Now, do us all a favour and get the hell outa here while you've still got some sheep left."

"Two days, you got, Ewen. Are you hearing me?" Holliger reiterated.

"That's not nearly long enough, and you know it," Augusta said. "Where can he take his sheep to?"

"He doesn't need his sheep, we'll take care of them," Holliger said with a sneer.

Brad was still watching the drama through his spyglass when Augusta accompanied Lord Ewen to the barn to collect his horse.

"I am very sorry about this, Charles," she said despairingly. "But what can I do? If only Sergeant Saunders

189

were here, but he seems to have deserted us."

It was on the tip of his tongue to tell her he'd seen the ranger but Ewen restrained himself. Brad had made it plain he wished as few people as possible to know he was around. Ewen waited while the stable-lad threw his saddle over his horse before adjusting the girth.

"I am not leaving, no matter what they say," he said stubbornly after the lad had left them.

"But what else can you do?" Augusta gripped his arm. "Those men hate you. They'll kill all your sheep and you as well if you don't go."

Without warning Lord Ewen took Augusta in his arms, moved her mourning veil aside and kissed her.

"Do you think I would leave you here on your own in this nest of rattlesnakes?" he said. "I repeat, I have no intention of leaving, and that is my final word."

He mounted his horse and rode

away, leaving Augusta standing open-mouthed in the deep shade of the barn.

From his hiding place, Brad observed with wry smile, the look of utter astonishment and joy on her face.

When she returned to the house, the guests were already departing. The unpleasant confrontation with Lord Ewen had unsettled everyone. Willi was engaged in deep conversation with Morgan Holliger when Augusta entered the room.

Everard Tuttle came bustling over to her. A dribble of wine ran down from the corner of the lawyer's mouth on to the soiled napkin he had neglected to remove. He had already helped himself to plenty of food and drink.

"I have brought your father's Will as you instructed, Miss von Faulkenburg," he said in his pompous voice. He looked pointedly at Morgan Holliger. "I shall read it as soon as all the mourners have gone."

Morgan Holliger took the hint and

taking up his hat, he came over to Augusta and said with a deferential smile, "With your permission I'll go now, Miss von Faulkenburg. Lord Ewen's behaviour was inexcusable. I am glad he had the decency to leave first. By the way, I must give my brother Lee's apologies for failing to attend this sad occasion. Unfortunately he was badly wounded yesterday by one of Lord Ewen's herders,"

"By the man he afterwards hung, I suppose?"

Augusta spoke with such heavy irony that even Holliger was taken aback, clearly unaware that she knew this.

"Look, what happened out on the range yesterday was a tragic mistake," he said. "Lee and his men had no intention of driving those sheep over the bluff. They only intended to teach Ewen a lesson. When the herder fired at Lee, the animals stampeded. The boys had no chance of stopping them."

"But was it necessary to hang the herder?" Augusta persisted to Holliger's obvious discomfiture.

"I told you, he took a shot at Lee. It was attempted murder. He got no more than he deserved."

"So, you are judge, jury and executioner without the inconvenience of a trial. God knows what my father would have thought about that. Good day to you, Morgan Holliger," Augusta said using all the not inconsiderable hauteur at her command.

As the chastened Holliger withdrew, she turned to Willi and Everard Tuttle.

"Very well, gentlemen, let us go into the baron's study and read the Will."

Fifteen minutes later, Willi von Faulkenburg emerged from the study, pale and shaking and headed straight for the door.

Augusta and Everard Tuttle came out after him.

"What has my father done?" Augusta exclaimed. "I knew there was insufficient capital to give me an annuity. But I never expected him to cut his only surviving son out of his Will completely."

"Your father is perhaps to be congratulated on his perspicacity," Tuttle said. "After all, as you quite rightly say, Willi never bothered to visit him and showed no interest in the business."

Tuttle coughed and shuffled uneasily from one foot to the other. He mopped his face with his handkerchief.

Augusta regarded him coldly. "Mr Tuttle, I have a feeling that there is something you haven't told me."

"I am sorry, Miss von Faulkenburg, but I do happen to know that Willi had er — gambled on inheriting the Iron Cross."

"What do you mean by *gambled*, Mr Tuttle?"

"That, literally, Miss von Faulkenburg. You see Willi staked all on the belief that he would inherit the Iron Cross."

Augusta stared at him. "What exactly do you mean when you say he *staked all*?"

Everard Tuttle blew his nose loudly.

"Exactly what I say, I'm afraid," he said through his handkerchief. "Your brother has gambled what he thought would be his inheritance away."

Augusta paled. "Oh the fool!" she exclaimed. She stared at Tuttle. "To whom does my brother owe this debt?"

"Morgan Holliger."

Augusta buried her face in her hands.

After a few moments she recovered her self-control and said, "Then I shall have to sell the Iron Cross to pay his debt."

Tuttle moved closer to Augusta and placed his pudgy hand protectively on her arm. "I may be able to be of assistance to you in your unfortunate plight, my dear Miss von Faulkenburg. First of all, rest assured, gambling debts are not enforceable in law."

"But a man has a duty to pay his debts!" Augusta exclaimed. "It is a matter of honour."

"With respect, that is your brother's problem, not yours. You must not be too hasty in going to his assistance, you have yourself to think of. Miss von Faulkenburg, you are now a wealthy young woman. I have admired your courage and fortitude ever since the day you arrived with your late father. Now I am an ambitious man, I don't intend to stay in this backwater for the rest of my life. It's my intention to stand for the next election to the state legislature. As my wife, you would be an ornament to that high office."

Augusta drew back. Tuttle recoiled as the look in her eyes condemned him to lower than a worm.

"You think to bribe me into marrying you with my father barely cold in his grave!" she exclaimed.

"I quite understand your reaction to my proposal. The moment is perhaps not the most opportune. But nevertheless I thought to make my feelings known to you. I should perhaps remind you that my standing in the legal profession is very high. Perhaps you will give it further thought when you are a little less distraught."

"Get out of this house, Mr Tuttle. Get out and never enter my door again."

Willi's abrupt departure followed by that of Everard Tuttle left Augusta on her own at the ranch apart from the servants. The sudden transition from having a throng of people about her to no one at all unsettled her and she went outside to inspect her father's grave.

The two cowhands who Pate had assigned to burying the baron were aligning a simple wooden cross over the grave when Augusta arrived.

The two men removed their hats and stood respectfully to one side when they saw Augusta.

"Will that be to your satisfaction, ma'am?" one of the men enquired.

Augusta nodded. "Yes, that is exactly what my father wanted." A sudden thought struck her. "Did you see which way my brother went?" she asked.

"You mean the guy who left in an all-fired hurry?" said one man. He winced as his companion gave him a painful clip on the shin with his spurred heel.

"I think that is the man," Augusta replied gravely.

"He went that-a-way," the man said, pointing towards Chanceville.

Chanceville? Now why would Willi want to ride back to Chanceville so quickly?

The reason came to her in a flash. Willi wasn't just going to Chanceville, he was running away for good!

She remembered how her father had pleaded with her to take care of him.

"Go and tell Manuel to put a horse to my buggy," she told one of the hands. "Tell him I am leaving in a few minutes."

* * *

Brad saw Willi emerge from the house and hurry round to the stable. The ranch hands had filled in the grave and were busy fixing a wooden cross over it. The hasty departure of the mourners had not been lost on him — it was plain that, although it was impossible for him to hear a word of what was said, the altercation between Lord Ewen and Willi had precipitated that.

As Willi emerged on horseback, Brad snapped his spy-glass shut and rose stiffly to his feet. As he walked back to where Blaze was grazing quietly he had a hunch that wherever Willi was going, from the distraught look on his face, it would be worthwhile to follow him.

"Hold it, right there, mister! Now keep your hands up and turn around real slow."

Holding his hands well clear of his sides, Brad turned to face a man he recognized as Ezra Pate, the Iron Cross foreman. He was holding a Colt. Beside him stood the same cowboy he'd had with him when they first met. He, too, was holding a revolver.

"Well, now, it looks like we ain't got rid of you after all," Pate said. "I guess Morgan Holliger will be very interested to know why you're still snoopin' round here."

"I'll bet he would," Brad agreed.

The younger man cocked his revolver. "Shall I kill him, boss?"

"No, you fool. Use your sense!" Pate exclaimed. "Not within sight and sound of the ranch. How the hell would we explain a gunshot? What would we do with a corpse on our hands? Besides which, this guy's a Ranger: kill him and you'll have the rest of his company on your trail forever. Leave the dirty work to Holliger and his boys. Now rope him up."

A few minutes later, Brad found himself trussed and tied to his horse.

That done, Pate said, "Now take him out to the cabin and keep guard. I'll send some of the boys out to spell you. Meantime I'll go talk with Holliger."

★ ★ ★

Willi had scarcely ridden a mile along the trail to Chanceville, when three men on horseback started out of the bushes, all of them holding revolvers.

"What's the all-fired hurry, Willi?"

Willi gasped as he recognized the rider in the centre of the group.

"Morgan, what are you doing here?"

"I might ask you the same question," Holliger said. He gestured to his men to withdraw. "Could it be that you're leavin' town?"

"Why should I want to do that?"

Holliger laughed harshly. "Oh come on, Willi, I ain't nobody's fool. Think I don't know what you're up to? All you gotta do is give Lawyer Tuttle the power of attorney to sell the ranch and get him to pass the money to you through a bank someplace back East. That way you dodge outa the debt you owe me. Well you can't pull a smartass trick like that on me, that's for sure."

"There's just one problem," Willi said. "Tuttle's read the Will, I've inherited nothing. My father has left the Iron Cross to Augusta."

Holliger's face turned thunderous. "You told me you were gonna inherit the lot. That was the basis on which we agreed to settle the debt."

"So I thought. But my father has ordered things otherwise."

Holliger raised his gun. "You stupid, blunderin' mutton-head, I oughta shoot you right now."

"If you do, you'll bury the chance of getting anything at all. As far as I am concerned it is a debt of honour and must one day be paid."

"You expect me to believe that?" Holliger said incredulously. "And how long is it gonna take?" He stroked his jaw thoughtfully. Suddenly a crafty smile lit up his saturnine features. "You could still inherit the Iron Cross," he said.

"How?"

"Well, the sudden death of your sister wouldn't be something your father would consider, would it?"

Willi froze as the implication of Holliger's words sank in.

"But you can't mean to murder Augusta!"

"Why not?" Holliger said callously. "I figure she's gonna marry Lord Ewen, so we gotta act quickly before that happens. The quicker she dies, the sooner you inherit the Iron Cross and the sooner it comes to me."

"I won't do it! Whatever I am, I'm no murderer."

"Who's talkin' 'bout murder?" Holliger asked innocently. "Haven't you ever heard of someone having a nasty accident?"

"I don't care how you put it. I won't be a party to killing my own sister."

"Well, you don't have to be. Knowing you, I guess you'd bungle it anyway."

"How are you going to do it?" Willi demanded.

Holliger shook his head. "I ain't gonna tell you fer sure. But in the meantime, my boys here are gonna take you someplace where you'll be outa harm's way. Now turn that hoss around and get movin'!"

★ ★ ★

It was late afternoon when Brad and his guard reached the cabin in the hills. The guard released him from his horse and frog marched him inside where he left him tied hand and foot.

"I'm gonna brew me some java," the guard said. "Don't think you'll be needin' any. I can't see Morgan Holliger wantin' you alive much longer."

A couple of hours passed during which Brad whiled away the time examining the efficiency with which he had been tied up and watching the similar efficiency of a solitary rat in its endless quest for food.

The sound of horses outside drew his attention. Listening intently, Brad overheard his guard greet a new arrival. Before long, the cabin door burst open and Willi von Faulkenburg was silhouetted in the doorway against the setting sun.

Willi was pushed unceremoniously inside and slumped down, dejectedly.

His arms were tied behind him and the guard secured his legs before leaving.

"So you didn't make it, Willi?" Brad said when they were alone.

Willi glared at Brad. "What are you talking about? Who are you? How do you know my name?"

"Your family are very good at asking questions, but not so hot at giving answers. My name's Brad Saunders and I'm a Texas Ranger investigating the sheep war in this county. I've already met your sister. Now if you wanna get outa here in one piece you'd better fill me in with what's been goin' on."

"My sister's in great danger," Willi said. "And I reckon it's all down to me."

Brad listened in grim silence as Willi recounted the story of his gambling disaster and the dire consequences threatened by Morgan Holliger.

"I guess I tried to outsmart him by leaving town after the Will was read, but it just didn't work. He and his boys were waiting for me before I could get away."

Brad looked at him with contempt. "You mean you were prepared to leave your sister to settle your debt to Morgan Holliger?"

"Surely, he wouldn't have asked *her* to settle my debt."

"Maybe not, but if I know your sister she'd do it as a matter of honour. Probably even agree to marry him to save your family's name."

Willi swallowed uncomfortably. "What else could I do? My one thought was to get away from Chanceville. And now Holliger's got me imprisoned here, I guess I've made a complete mess of everything."

"One thing is certain," Brad observed. "If your sister is to have any chance of survival, I'm gonna have to get out of here — fast."

Willi looked up in alarm. "But what about me?"

"Aw, shut up!" Brad snarled. "You should have thought of that before you got into this mess."

After an unappetising meal of congealed beans and tepid coffee brought in by one of the three guards, their arms, which had been released to enable them to eat were retied and they spent the night in increasing discomfort. The logs from which the cabin was built seemed to radiate more heat than ever after the heat of the day and they had been left only one panikin of brackish water between them from which they were compelled to lap like dogs. It was plain to Brad that although his own iron constitution was coping with the situation, Willi's wasn't. By dawn, he was restless and feverish.

The door opened and one of the guards appeared with more beans and weak coffee dregs.

"This room service ain't goin' on for you much longer," the guard said sarcastically. "I guess you'll be pleased to know that we're expectin' Mr Holliger soon. No doubt he'll have figured a way to get rid of you."

"You've got a sick man on your hands," Brad said, nodding towards Willi. "He ain't bearing up to being kept roped up like this. I don't figure Mr Holliger is gonna take it kindly iffen he dies, it might get in the way of his plans."

The guard went outside and after a brief discussion with his companions, he returned and released Willi's hands and loosened the binding round his legs. Whilst he was doing this, the sound of approaching riders drew his attention.

Suddenly the cabin door opened and Morgan Holliger was silhouetted in the opening. He was in a towering rage.

He walked straight over to where Brad was lying and kicked him savagely in the ribs.

"I figured you'd had the sense to leave this area well alone," he said.

"I was sent here to do a job," Brad replied. "And I'm gonna do it. Your brother, Lee, escaped custody the other day. I take it you're harbouring him?"

Holliger unleashed another kick.

"Don't think you're ever gonna arrest Lee, Ranger, because you're not." His expression became crafty. "Say now, I wonder just what you've been up to this last couple days?"

"Enough to know that if you go through with what you're planning, you'll be on a charge of attempted murder. That's apart from running a relay station for rustled cattle along with Ezra Pate and unlawfully allowin' your men to slaughter Lord Ewen's stock, wound one of his herders and hang another."

"Say now, ain't you just the clever lawman?" Holliger sneered. "You can't prove any of those charges. But I guess you know too much. What a shame you ain't gonna live to tell the tale."

"Kill me and you'll have the rangers on your trail," Brad warned.

"D'you think I'm stupid enough to kill you?" Holliger jeered.

"I figured it was you who tried to kill me on the way to Chanceville," Brad retorted.

"Sure, sure, I did. Lucky for you that lousy sheepherder was there."

"Diego is dead," Brad said quietly. "And I want the guy who did it."

"I'll bet you do. But wishing's as far as you're gonna get. In between times you're gonna take a little trip over the bluff."

"I thought you said you weren't gonna kill me?" Brad said.

Holliger nodded. "No, I ain't. My men are gonna take you up there and somehow you're gonna take a tumble over the edge. When Hall comes, it's gonna look like you was investigatin' what happened to those sheep and fell yourself. Why should anyone want to enlighten him? You see, I've learned a lot just lately. I've come round to realizin' you can achieve more by accident than by blowing a man's brains out."

"Just what accident have you planned

for Miss von Faulkenburg?" Brad enquired.

Holliger glanced at Willi. "I see he's been talkin'. Well I guess there's no harm in tellin' you. She's ridden into town, on a wild goose chase lookin' for him. I reckon on her way back tomorrow, that buggy of hers will overturn. There's many a law-abidin' person gone to their Maker that way."

Which was absolutely true.

With that Holliger went outside where Brad heard him giving orders for Willi to be held under guard outside the cabin under the shade of a tree during the day and be given food and plenty of water. Whilst this was happening, Brad shuffled across to where Willi lay. To his relief he opened his eyes and smiled weakly at Brad.

"That man is insane," Willi muttered. "What can we do?"

"Quickly, man, undo this rope on my wrists, before they come back for you," Brad said urgently.

With an effort, Willi picked at the knot until he untied it. Brad freed himself and then said, "Now put it back. Just enough to make it look as though it's tied. Hurry, man, fer God's sake, it's the only chance we've got to save your sister!"

11

DAWN was streaking the sky, promising another hot day when two of the guards came to collect Brad from the cabin.

One of them cut his legs free, but he didn't bother to check his wrists.

"Well, Ranger, I guess *you* won't be needin' breakfast," he said as his *compadre* placed another mess of congealed beans and mug of tepid coffee beside Willi.

Brad ignored the taunt as he rose stiffly to his feet and the two guards escorted him outside, with his hands still tied behind him. Blaze was ready waiting and, without checking his bonds, together the guards heaved Brad into the saddle. Mounting their own horses, they led him out of the valley in a direction he recognized as heading towards the bluffs.

After two hours of steady riding, they arrived at their goal and Brad mentally braced himself knowing that when the moment came, he would have only one chance . . . and the problem was, guessing just exactly when that chance might be.

He had had plenty of time to study his captors during the long ride. Both of them were hard-faced, seasoned men used to living on whichever side of the law suited them. To try to catch such men as these unawares was hopeless and could only end in disaster.

The men allowed their horses to pick their way across the rocky terrain leading towards the edge of the bluff. As they drew closer, the stench of decay from the carcasses of the dead sheep lying in heaps at the foot of the bluff tainted the warm breeze.

"This is far enough, I reckon," one of the men said.

His companion regarded Blaze with a gleam in his eye.

"I reckon drivin' both man and hoss

over this bluff is a waste of a damn good hoss," he said.

His companion nodded.

"Best keep the hoss, that's fer sure."

Both men dismounted and stood by watching as Brad did the same with difficulty, ostensibly hampered by the bonds loosely securing his wrists.

"Say, there's been something buggin' me," one of the guards said. "D'you remember the guy who gave us that pastin' instead of his wallet the other night in Chanceville?"

Brad remembered it well, but he gave no sign of it.

"Uh-huh. Tell me about it," the other man said with a grimace. "I'd had so many whiskeys I lost count."

"Well, I reckon this is him."

"Now, ain't that a stroke of luck! An' this time we ain't too drunk to handle him."

The two men seized Brad by the arms and frog marched him to the very edge of the bluff.

"Take a good look down yonder,

Ranger," one of the men said with a sneer. "Take a good, long look, because that's all you're gonna get before you hit them rocks."

For a brief moment Brad looked below him at the gigantic landslip of broken rocks over which lay the carcasses of sheep heaped in piles with buzzards still circling over them contesting the pickings with coyotes. Some of the animals had already been picked clean and the bones gleamed in the reflected sunlight.

"Hasn't the condemned man got any last words?" one of the men said sarcastically.

Even as he was speaking, Brad was easing the bonds clear of his wrists, praying his muscles hadn't stiffened too much to prevent him doing what he knew he had to do.

"He don't talk much, does he?" the other man said. "Well all right, Ranger, we'll see you in hell . . . "

At the instant the two men firmed their hold on him and pushed forward,

Brad dug both heels in and leaned backwards. At the same time he wrapped both his freed arms around the waists of the two men and transferred his weight forward with all his strength, using the momentum they created to propel them headlong over the edge of the bluff.

It seemed like an eternity before their agonized shrieks ceased to echo from the face of the bluff and attenuated into a ghastly silence.

Brad fell forwards on to his hands and knees like a supplicant. He remained thus, transfixed for several moments, overcome by the enormity of what he had done.

It took Blaze's gentle whicker to bring him back to reality. He rose unsteadily to his feet and reached out for the animal's muzzle. As the horse drew close he embraced it, drawing inner strength from the only creature he trusted in the whole world.

As the seconds passed, his iron self-discipline slowly returned and a clear priority began to establish itself in his mind. Augusta von Faulkenburg's life was in danger and he was the only one who could do anything about it.

Mechanically, he unsaddled the other two horses and left them to shift for themselves. Before mounting Blaze, he checked his Winchester was still in its scabbard.

Without a last look back, he rode away from the bluff which had seen so much needless slaughter of man and beast. Instinctively he knew the only way forward was action. Past experience taught him that brooding could send a man mad. For him, this place would always carry the chilling aura of a battlefield. During the Civil War he had fought in many a fray and killed men whose names he would never know.

And at the foot of the bluff lay the broken bodies of two more.

★ ★ ★

Augusta could find no trace of Willi in Chanceville. From the moment she found the livery stable did not hold his horse, she had her doubts. He hadn't checked in at Weaver's Hotel, which was his usual haunt. Frank Brock, the only citizen she could trust, hadn't seen him either.

"But he must be here somewhere!" Augusta exclaimed.

"I take it you are aware of Willi's financial situation," Brock said tactfully.

Augusta nodded. "I know he is a gambler. Unfortunately for him, my father's Will has not made it possible for him to pay his debt to Morgan Holliger."

"I see. Indeed, the matter is worse than I expected. That explains why he has disappeared," Brock said.

"I cannot believe it!" Augusta exclaimed. "A von Faulkenburg does not try to evade a debt of honour."

"Perhaps he thought that discretion was the better part of *noblesse oblige*," Brock replied.

"But Willi couldn't survive outdoors the way the cowboys do," she argued. "He isn't a Westerner. When he served in the Prussian Army he had a clerical job at a supply base. What do you suggest I do, Mr Brock?"

The banker undertook to investigate Willi's more disreputable haunts, including the Graveyard Saloon, but neither Carter Rankin nor the ever-discreet Alabama Rose were able to help.

"I don't think he is in town, Miss von Faulkenburg," Brock told her later that evening. "My advice is that you stay the night here at the hotel and go back to the ranch tomorrow. In the meantime I will keep an eye out for him."

After spending the following morning making more fruitless enquiries, Augusta decided to take Brock's advice and return to the Iron Cross. After breakfasting alone in her room at Weaver's Hotel, she went to collect her buggy from the livery. As she crossed the dusty street, she did not see the only man in Chanceville who knew where Willi was. He was standing on the sidewalk, watching her as intently as a cat watches a mouse.

As Augusta shook the reins and urged her horse forward, Morgan Holliger stamped on the butt of the cigar he was smoking, moved out of the deep shade afforded by the boardwalk and unhitched his own mount.

★ ★ ★

All Brad could do was backtrack the Chanceville trail from the vicinity of the Iron Cross, keeping an eye out for Augusta's buggy. As he cantered along, he noticed several spots where a buggy might overturn, with serious consequences for its occupant. Every trail in the West had its tally of unfortunate accidents. Circumspect as he was, he saw no sign of Morgan Holliger and the closer he came to Chanceville, his spirits rose.

Five miles out, he caught sight of the dust cloud of an approaching vehicle. He urged Blaze forward and was mightily relieved to see that it was indeed, Augusta in her buggy.

"Good day to you, ma'am," Brad said as he reined in alongside her.

"Sergeant Saunders!" she exclaimed. "Why, everyone said you'd left Chanceville."

"I guess they were wrong," he replied.

"They most certainly were."

Brad wheeled round as another voice spoke behind him.

"Oh Morgan, it's you?" Augusta exclaimed. "But why are you holding a gun?"

"Why I guess the ranger here could tell you that," Holliger said with a harsh laugh. "But before he does, perhaps he might explain how he comes to be here?"

"It's you who have the explaining to do, Herr Holliger. Drop your gun this instant, or you are a dead man."

The command carried the ruthless authority of one used to being obeyed.

Slowly Holliger did as he was bidden. As he did so, the bushes parted at the side of the trail and a rider emerged holding a rifle.

"Charles!" Augusta exclaimed. "How did you come to be here?"

"After what happened yesterday I decided to call on you. Your foreman told me you had gone into town to look for your brother, so I thought to ride in and offer you my assistance."

If it sounded thinner than tissue paper, Augusta gave no sign of it. But Brad was becoming thoroughly convinced that Ewen's decision to stay was as much influenced by his regard for her as for his sheep.

While his attention was distracted, Holliger suddenly spurred his horse forward in a bid for freedom. Lord Ewen reacted swiftly. Holliger had scarcely ridden a hundred yards, before the Englishman caught up with him.

With a snarl, Holliger turned in his

saddle to fight off his pursuer. But he was fighting a trained cavalryman. Ewen shoulder-charged his horse against Holliger's, knocking him clean out of the saddle. Holliger fell heavily, hitting his head, and lay dazed.

"You seem quite handy at knocking guys out," Brad remarked dryly as he drew up alongside.

Lord Ewen whirled his horse round and grinned. "The wretched fellow is lucky I wasn't carrying a lance, or he would have been squealing like a stuck pig."

Brad tied Holliger's wrists securely behind him. When he had finished, he sought and found Holliger's pearl-handled Colt, checked the loads and dropped it into his own holster. By this time Holliger was showing signs of coming round.

"What are you doing about this man's threat to run you off the range?" Augusta asked Lord Ewen.

"I don't give a fig for that," Lord Ewen replied.

"Don't be too sure, Ewen," Holliger said. He had come round and was rubbing an open wound on his scalp. "My brother is gettin' the boys ready. When they move in there won't be another sheep left."

"He won't trouble me."

Brad smiled inwardly at the confidence in Ewen's voice. Both he and Augusta made Holliger, despite his strutting arrogance, seem small beer. These blue-bloods were a breed all their own.

"I wish I knew where Willi is," Augusta said.

"Why do you bother about him so?" Lord Ewen asked her. "He has shown very little concern for you."

"Wilhelm is my flesh and blood," Augusta replied. "It was my father's last wish that I do not abandon him."

Lord Ewen bowed. "May I tender my sincerest apologies, Miss von Faulkenburg. It was very remiss of me to speak of your brother in that manner."

"I accept your apology, my lord."

For a few brief, fascinating moments, Brad watched as the etiquette of the salons and courts of Europe, honed by centuries of tradition, was enacted before him.

"I know where Willi is," Brad said. "Holliger intercepted him on his way into town. He's got him holed up in a cabin in yonder hills. Pate had me held there too, until this morning."

"What has Mr Pate got to do with this?" Augusta demanded.

"Miss von Faulkenburg, I'm sorry to tell you that your foreman is involved up to his neck in rustling cattle," Brad replied. "An' Holliger is in cahoots with him, too."

Seeing Augusta's puzzled expression, Brad went on, "What I mean, ma'am, is that your foreman and Holliger are both in it together."

Augusta stared at Brad. "Are you saying that Mr Pate has been deceiving my father?"

"I'm afraid so, ma'am."

Augusta rounded on Holliger.

"And you had no right to abduct my brother."

"He owes me money," Holliger snapped. "A little matter of fifty thousand dollars he lost in a poker game."

"Gambling debts are not recognized in law," Brad said.

"I'm not talking' about law, I'm talking about a debt of honour," Holliger said.

"Don't you dare speak of honour, sir!" Lord Ewen snapped.

"So? I always understood you blue-bloods had a keen sense of such things," Holliger retorted.

"Quit arguin'," Brad broke in. "It ain't gettin' us nowhere." He turned to Lord Ewen. "Come on, let's you and me ride out to the cabin and free Willi."

"I'll come, too," Augusta said.

"There ain't no need," Brad told her. "Where we're going ain't buggy country, that's fer sure."

"That is no problem," Augusta

replied. "We'll call back at the ranch and I will ride Wotan."

Brad could see her mind was made up.

"What are we going to do with him?" Lord Ewen asked, indicating Holliger with all the distaste he would a mangy dog.

"He's comin' with us."

As they moved off, Brad fell in alongside Holliger.

"How the hell did you escape?" Holliger said with a snarl. "I left some of my best men guarding you."

Brad's face turned grim. "Let's say two of 'em happened an accident."

Augusta's face was set hard as they entered the Iron Cross yard.

"Manuel, where is Mr Pate?" she demanded.

"*Señorita*, he is not here," the boy replied as he commenced the task of unhitching the horse from her buggy.

"Leave that, just saddle Wotan," Augusta snapped.

The boy ran to do her bidding and by

the time Augusta reappeared wearing a blouse and her divided riding skirt he had Wotan saddled and waiting.

Two hours later during which Brad's initial opinion of Augusta's riding ability was further enhanced, the little cavalcade mounted the rimrock from which they could look down on the hidden valley which held the cabin.

"How can you be sure that Mr Pate is a rustler?" Augusta asked Brad as they looked down on the small groups of cattle dotted about the valley.

"I have sufficient proof to stand up in a court of law," Brad replied.

"Except perhaps in Chanceville," Lord Ewen remarked dryly.

"Rustling cattle's one thing, raisin' sheep's another," Brad reminded him.

"Point taken," Lord Ewen replied.

Brad viewed the situation through his spy-glass.

"Pate is there, with three other guys," he muttered. "They must be holdin' Willi inside. I'll stake my last dollar Pate's been doin' some more rebranding."

"We must rescue Willi," Augusta said urgently.

"How about a night attack?" Lord Ewen offered. "Take the beggars by surprise, what?"

Brad shot a half-amused glance at him. This was the soldier talking now.

"I ain't got time fer that. Now, this is my business and here's what we're gonna do," he replied.

A few minutes later, Lord Ewen left Brad to ride further round the head of the valley and Brad waited until through his glass he could see he had reached a point nearly opposite him. As soon as Ewen gave the pre-arranged signal of waving his hat, Brad set about cutting Holliger's wrists free.

"Now remember," Brad said to Augusta. "You stay up here until it's over." He gave her the spy-glass. "You can watch what's happening through this."

He edged his horse over to Holliger.

"Now just you ride down ahead of me nice and natural like I'm one of your hired hands."

"You ain't gonna get away with this," Holliger said. "My boys will gun you down once they get wise."

"Tell me, Holliger, you ever heard of *la ley de fuga*?"

"Yeah, it's old Spanish law where a prisoner can be shot if there's a rescue attempt."

"OK, so now you know where you stand," Brad said.

"But that ain't the law in Texas," Holliger complained.

"It was McNelly's law," Brad told him. "It's good enough for me and as far as I know, his successor has never rescinded it. Now get movin'. And remember, you just tell your boys to give themselves up and no one is gonna get hurt."

At a prod from Brad, Holliger set his horse in motion and kept ahead of him as they rode down the slope to the cabin.

Through the spy-glass, Augusta saw one of her hired hands appear outside the cabin. Where was Charles? The hired hand turned to call back into the cabin and another man she recognized as Pate, along with two others appeared.

Thirty paces away, to his left, Brad caught sight of a slight movement near a water trough. Praise be Ewen was there, and not a moment too late.

"Hey Morgan, what kept you so long?" Pate called out.

"Hell's teeth, it's the Ranger!"

The guy who'd been assigned as a guard had recognized him!

"What are you waiting for? Wipe him out!" Holliger shouted.

Suddenly, to Augusta, it seemed that the whole field of view through the spy-glass had become a blur of movement. Holliger spurred his horse, wrenching the bridle down to force the animal to one side. The man who had recognized Brad made a grab for his gun but too late as Brad hauled out his borrowed weapon and fired. Augusta gasped as the slug hit the man full in the chest and he staggered forward, permanently out of the reckoning.

Suddenly Charles came into view. He was on foot, rifle in hand, at right angles to Brad. His appearance distracted Holliger's horse which shied away just as Pate and his companions drew and fired.

Holliger, still fighting desperately to retain control of his mount, took the full force of the volley fired by Pate and his companions. He toppled out of the saddle and flopped on to the ground with his horse on top of him.

Brad wheeled Blaze about and snapped off a shot. The slug hit Pate, knocking him over backwards into the cabin doorway. Ewen fired with ruthless accuracy, killing one of Pate's *compadres* instantly.

By now, the remaining man had taken refuge behind a barrel which offered little protection to the firepower of Ewen's rifle. After a brief exchange, a bandana was waved on the end of a six-gun.

"I do believe he is surrendering," Lord Ewen called out to Brad.

Which was indeed the case. The deaths of Holliger and Pate and the hired hands had knocked all the fight out of him.

After a few seconds of savage fighting, it was all over. Augusta snapped the spy-glass shut, mounted her horse and rode down the slope to the cabin.

"Was all this killing necessary?" she exclaimed in horror.

"I don't think it went quite as we planned," Lord Ewen admitted.

"Holliger had every chance to tell his men to surrender and he chose not to," Brad said quietly.

Augusta stared at him. "I do not believe you. I think you wanted this to happen. You call yourself a lawman and you are no better than the men you have killed."

"Augusta, I think you are being less than fair," Lord Ewen said as Brad turned away in disgust.

"So where is my brother?" Augusta demanded.

Brad led the way inside the cabin. Augusta gasped when she saw Willi lying bound in the corner. All her revulsion at what had just happened outside evaporated.

"To think they kept you here, tethered like a dog," she exclaimed as Brad cut Willi free.

"Thank you, Sergeant Saunders. I never thought I would see you again," Willi said, as he rubbed the life back into his wrists.

Augusta listened in mounting horror as Willi recounted Holliger's plan to have Brad hurled to his death over the bluff.

"How did you ever come to be involved with a monster like him?" was all she could say.

Willi blinked against the bright sunshine as he emerged from the cabin. Augusta noticed he seemed to have aged ten years since she had last seen him. All his cockiness, the arrogant self assurance had gone.

Meantime, Brad set the hired hand to the task of burying all the corpses with the exception of Holliger which he placed over the saddle of a spare horse. That done he addressed himself to finding his stolen Peacemaker and replaced it for Holliger's weapon. He then took time out to give Augusta and Lord Ewen a brief exposition of Pate's rustling operation and how it was effected.

"What happens now?" Ewen asked him.

"You take Augusta and Willi with you back to the Iron Cross."

"And you?"

"I still got me some unfinished business and whilst there's daylight left I'd like to complete it."

"You're having a busy day. I take it you mean Lee Holliger?"

Brad nodded. "He escaped from my custody, I want him back."

As Brad went to recover Blaze,

Augusta walked with him. As he put a foot in a stirrup, she caught him by the arm.

"Sergeant Saunders, here is your spy-glass."

"Why, thank you, ma'am. I was quite forgettin' it," he said.

She hesitated. "Lord Ewen has just told me that Morgan Holliger was killed by his own men after he called upon them to fire at you. I must apologize for what I said just now. It was unforgivable."

"It was understandable," Brad replied. "I never intended for you to have to watch all that gunplay."

"You are a very brave man, Sergeant Saunders. In the Prussian Army they would have awarded you the Iron Cross."

Before Brad could reply, she moved close to him and kissed him on the cheek.

"Thank you for rescuing Willi," she said with a smile so sincere it left him more confused than ever.

12

IT was evening when Brad rode alone through the gate of the Lazy Y. There was no one about and the smell of cooking meat and coffee indicated it was pretty close to chow time. As he rode past the cookhouse, a man poked his grizzled head out and shouted, "Tell 'em to come and get it . . ."

The words died on his lips when he saw the horse behind Brad carrying the corpse.

"Who the hell yuh got there, mister?" he demanded.

"I want to see Lee Holliger," Brad said. "Where will I find him?"

"I'm right here," a voice said.

Brad turned to see Lee coming down the steps from the stoop at the main entrance to the ranch house. As he did so, he was joined by a dozen hands spilling out of the bunkhouse into the yard.

"What are you doin' here, Ranger?" Lee called out. "I thought my brother had warned you off."

Brad released the tether holding the other horse and directed the animal towards Holliger.

"What's goin' on? Who's this?" Lee exclaimed as he grabbed the horse's bridle.

"Take a good look," Brad said.

The yard fell silent as Lee inspected the face of the corpse.

His face turned pale. "Why it's Morgan!"

His hand moved to his hip, but Brad already had his Peacemaker trained on him. Faced with over a dozen men, he was taking no chances.

"Did you do this?" Lee shouted.

"I did it," Brad assured him. "He died whilst trying to escape arrest."

"Arrest for what?" Lee demanded.

"Attempted murder," Brad replied.

"I don't believe you. I reckon you've

laid up and bushwhacked him."

"In that case why am I here?"

Lee stared at Brad. When he didn't answer, Brad went on, "I think you know why. You escaped from my custody the other night in Chanceville."

"I didn't!" Lee protested. "Your sheepherdin' sidekick slugged you and gave me the key to the cell."

"To save you from bein' burned alive by your brother's actions," Brad said. "Now get your horse, you're back under arrest."

Lee backed off and looked across at his men. "Say now, how are you gonna do that?" he jeered.

Pointing his Peacemaker firmly at Lee, Brad said, "These guys aren't gonna do anything to stop me."

"You hear that, boys?"

"We hear it," one man said. "If one of us draws, you're a dead man along with your brother."

"And if I die, Miss Augusta von Faulkenburg knows exactly where I am," Brad said. "She will inform the ranger headquarters back in San Antonio. Boys, Morgan Holliger is already dead. The killing has to stop sooner or later. I reckon the Lazy Y is finished. It's time you called it a day."

"I reckon he's right," an older man said. "I signed up to punch cattle not harass women and sheepherders. Boys, Morgan Holliger is dead. It don't do to upset the rangers, that's fer sure. I'm gonna find me another employer."

"But what about me?" Lee shouted. "If Morgan's dead, I'm your boss now."

"No you ain't," said a voice from the crowd. "If this ranger don't take you, another one will. And when that happens, who's gonna pay our wages?"

There was a general murmur of agreement, the tension relaxed and the men dispersed, leaving Lee standing open-mouthed in the middle of the yard.

★ ★ ★

"Well now, gentlemen, I guess you'll have realized that recent events have changed our way of thinking," Jackson Venn said.

Venn was chairing a meeting of the Chanceville Cattleman's Association in a smoke-filled private room at Weaver's Hotel. There were a dozen other cattlemen present, and Augusta von Faulkenburg who was dressed in black in mourning for her father. Frank Brock, who financed most of their operations was there, too, as were Lance Quirk, the stage and freight-line owner, and Everard Tuttle, the lawyer, all of whom had a vested interest in the industry.

Sheriff Grant with his arm in a sling, sat next to Brad. On the other side sat the slim figure of Lord Ewen.

"Now I'll level with you," Venn continued. "I was just as opposed to sheep-rearing in Texas as every other cattleman in this room. But I can't go along with violence and intimidation on the scale that has been going on in our area. It was the law's bounden duty to stop it and it's my regret it got so out of hand it cost several people their lives. I do feel we owe a debt of gratitude to our own sheriff and also to Sergeant Brad Saunders."

Amid the polite round of applause, Brad rose to say, "May I say that, born and raised in the Panhandle, I also was of the same opinion as yourselves about raising sheep and at first nothing would have pleased me more than to persuade Lord Ewen to leave. But I am a lawman and it's my job to uphold the law. I cannot believe that these events were the result of the official policy of this association and Mr Brock assures me that it was the financial state of the Lazy Y which drove Morgan Holliger to act the way he did."

Brad saw several grizzled heads nod in acknowledgment of his tact in handling a delicate situation.

Brock held up his hand. On the chairman's nod, he rose and said, "What Sergeant Saunders says is true.

The Lazy Y is now bankrupt and I shall be putting it on the market as soon as the legal proceedings have been completed."

There was a stir, as Lord Ewen indicated his wish to speak.

"I would like to inform this meeting that the Scottish-based investment company which backs me has indicated its willingness to go into cattle ranching. I intend to press for them to purchase the Lazy Y and to run a combined cattle and sheep raising operation side-by-side as a formal experiment to prove that it works."

There were dollar signs reflected in everyone's eyes when Lance Quirk rose and said, "Gentlemen, I say there is more money to be made from the peaceful economic development of this area than fighting among ourselves."

Everard Tuttle rubbed his pudgy hands in anticipation as he added, "The state senate will no doubt be vastly impressed with our level of co-operation with foreign investors."

The meeting broke into an excited babble of conversation until Venn called it to order.

"Mr Brock?"

"Lest any of you still feel inclined to reject this business out of hand," Brock said. "Please remember that the investment of money into this area can bring it nothing but greater prosperity."

"What are you proposing, Frank?" Venn growled.

"That this Cattleman's Association abandons any hostility to Lord Ewen forthwith."

★ ★ ★

As Brad made his way out of the crowded hotel foyer, Augusta von Faulkenburg came over to him.

"Where are you going now, Sergeant Saunders?"

"Why, back to San Antonio, I guess."

"It is too late for you to do that. Lord Ewen is staying on in town.

Would you escort me back to the Iron Cross? There is a little matter I would like us to settle."

Brad smiled. What was the point in arguing with a woman like Augusta von Faulkenburg?

The journey passed pleasantly enough. The dinner prepared by the Iron Cross cook and served by candlelight was excellent. Augusta, soberly dressed in black with a ruby brooch at her neck, was living proof that a woman could look attractive without going to extremes. She proved to be an excellent conversationalist and Brad found himself telling more of his past than he was accustomed to.

"What will your brother do now?" he enquired.

"Lord Ewen has offered Willi a position."

"Will he take it?"

"I hope so. It will enable me to fulfil my father's last wish."

"Do you think perhaps Morgan Holliger's death and Lee's eventual trial have shown him the error of his ways?"

Augusta nodded. "I believe it has. He certainly seems a changed man. Perhaps he will make something of his life now."

"Mind if I smoke?" Brad asked as the servant brought coffee.

"Of course not," Augusta said. "Abigail, bring my father's cigar box, will you?

"You have certainly travelled a great deal. Do you think you will settle down one day?" she asked him as he poured brandy into her glass.

"Maybe," he said enigmatically.

The evening was drawing to a close when they went out on to the stoop. Brad flicked his cigar ash into the night. Over in the barn the horses stamped and snorted.

"Sergeant Saunders, I said there was a matter I wished to settle between us," Augusta said.

Brad inclined his head towards her.

"Do you remember the first day we

met, how I admired your horse?"

"Sure, I remember. You were riding Wotan."

Augusta slipped her arm inside Brad's. Suddenly, her stiff Teutonic reserve fell away. "Do you remember how you said you would back your horse against mine?"

He smiled to himself. "Why, I guess so."

"Well, tomorrow morning at dawn, when Blaze is rested, would you race me on Wotan?"

"And what is the prize for the winner?" he asked her.

"That is for the winner to decide," she replied lightly.

In the dusk, Brad could have sworn she was blushing.

★ ★ ★

There was just the two of them, side by side, sitting astride two magnificent stallions, one a bay, the other as white as snow when dawn burst over the distant hills painting the great canvas of sky with profligate slashes of gold, crimson and yellow.

Both riders waited as though transfixed until the initial splendour had passed away into the broader light of a new day. Behind them, through the shade of scrub oaks, Pilson's Creek babbled over its bedrock.

"So what is the course?" Brad enquired.

Wotan was skittish, anxious to be away, but Augusta held him with masterly control. Blaze was sweating, almost as though anticipating the oncoming battle of Titans.

Augusta was wearing a white blouse with sleeves ruffed at the cuffs and her divided leather riding skirt. Determination was etched on her face as she pointed to the skyline.

"Do you see that hill? At its foot there is an oak. We circle the oak and return here."

"How far is that?"

"It is five miles. The ground falls

and rises but it is fair and there are no obstacles. Are you ready?"

Brad nodded and the animals moved off, easily into a steady canter down the slope. The pace slowly increased and maintained as they hit the rise, dust lifting in a cloud behind them.

Blaze was first past the oak tree, with Wotan at a length behind, but Augusta touched him lightly with her spurs to draw him level as soon as they were clear.

The pace was quickening now. Brad sensed that Augusta's horse was bred for stamina but lacked the daily hard grind that Blaze was used to. Wotan would finish strongly if Blaze didn't take the pace out of him.

Accordingly, Brad slowly but surely began to wind up the pace, always keeping Blaze a neck, a head — sometimes even half a length in front. Augusta had been right — the ground was fair and there was no need to guide the animals into better ground. This was a race where genuine pace would receive its just reward.

As they neared the finish, one thing hovered in the back of Brad's mind. What would he claim as his prize if Blaze won?

The horses were neck and neck as they breasted the final rise to the finish. Had Blaze taken the pace out of Wotan? A touch of the spurs produced a final surge of power but to Brad's amazement Wotan responded, drew level and over the final yards pulled half a length clear.

"That was magnificent!"

Augusta turned to Brad, her eyes shining as they led the horses gently down the slope to the creek.

They unsaddled the animals, flung saddle blankets over them and allowed them to walk free.

"Well?" Brad said. "You said the winner could name their own prize."

Augusta laughed. Brad realized it was the first time she had done so since they had met and it took years off her.

"Tell me, Sergeant Saunders, what you would have asked for and I will grant it as my wish," she said.

For answer he took her in his arms and kissed her. Her response was surprisingly uninhibited. It was clearly what she had had in mind all along.

After a while, she withdrew from him and moved a lock of hair away from her cheek with a curiously disarming gesture.

"I am very sorry, Brad — I may call you Brad, may I?"

He nodded. For a few brief moments her defences had come down. He knew instinctively what she was going to say.

"This has been very wrong. You must excuse me, I think perhaps the events of the last few days have distracted me. I do not wish to convey the impression I am a woman of low morals."

"I never thought that for a minute," Brad reassured her.

"That is very honorable of you, Sergeant Saunders, but I have to tell you I am engaged to marry Lord Ewen."

Noblesse oblige had reasserted itself, for after all Augusta was the daughter of Baron von Faulkenburg . . .

★ ★ ★

Bone-weary, Brad dismounted and tethered Blaze to the hitching post outside Hall's office in San Antonio. He mounted the boardwalk and went inside.

The ranger captain looked up as Brad entered the room.

"Ah, Sergeant Saunders," he said with a smile. "You're just the man I'm lookin' for. I didn't think that little business at Chanceville would take you very long."

TOP HAND
Wade Everett

The Broken T was big. But no ranch is big enough to let a man hide from himself.

GUN WOLVES OF LOBO BASIN
Lee Floren

The Feud was a blood debt. When Smoke Talbot found the outlaws who gunned down his folks he aimed to nail their hide to the barn door.

SHOTGUN SHARKEY
Marshall Grover

The westbound coach carrying the indomitable Larry and Stretch headed for a shooting showdown.

FIGHTING RAMROD
Charles N. Heckelmann

Most men would have cut their losses, but Frazer counted the bullets in his guns and said he'd soak the range in blood before he'd give up another inch of what was his.

LONE GUN
Eric Allen

Smoke Blackbird had been away too long. The Lequires had seized the Blackbird farm, forcing the Indians and settlers off, and no one seemed willing to fight! He had to fight alone.

THE THIRD RIDER
Barry Cord

Mel Rawlins wasn't going to let anything stand in his way. His father was murdered, his two brothers gone. Now Mel rode for vengeance.

ARIZONA DRIFTERS
W. C. Tuttle

When drifting Dutton and Lonnie Steelman decide to become partners they find that they have a common enemy in the formidable Thurston brothers.

TOMBSTONE
Matt Braun

Wells Fargo paid Luke Starbuck to outgun the silver-thieving stagecoach gang at Tombstone. Before long Luke can see the only thing bearing fruit in this eldorado will be the gallows tree.

HIGH BORDER RIDERS
Lee Floren

Buckshot McKee and Tortilla Joe cut the trail of a border tough who was running Mexican beef into Texas. They stopped the smuggler in his tracks.

BRETT RANDALL, GAMBLER
E. B. Mann

Larry Day had the choice of running away from the law or of assuming a dead man's place. No matter what he decided he was bound to end up dead.

THE GUNSHARP
William R. Cox

The Eggerleys weren't very smart. They trained their sights on Will Carney and Arizona's biggest blood bath began.

THE DEPUTY OF SAN RIANO
Lawrence A. Keating and
Al. P. Nelson

When a man fell dead from his horse, Ed Grant was spotted riding away from the scene. The deputy sheriff rode out after him and came up against everything from gunfire to dynamite.

FARGO: MASSACRE RIVER
John Benteen

The ambushers up ahead had now blocked the road. Fargo's convoy was a jumble, a perfect target for the insurgents' weapons!

SUNDANCE: DEATH IN THE LAVA
John Benteen

The Modoc's captured the wagon train and its cargo of gold. But now the halfbreed they called Sundance was going after it . . .

HARSH RECKONING
Phil Ketchum

Five years of keeping himself alive in a brutal prison had made Brand tough and careless about who he gunned down . . .

FARGO: PANAMA GOLD
John Benteen

With foreign money behind him, Buckner was going to destroy the Panama Canal before it could be completed. Fargo's job was to stop Buckner.

FARGO:
THE SHARPSHOOTERS
John Benteen

The Canfield clan, thirty strong were raising hell in Texas. Fargo was tough enough to hold his own against the whole clan.

PISTOL LAW
Paul Evan Lehman

Lance Jones came back to Mustang for just one thing — revenge! Revenge on the people who had him thrown in jail.

HELL RIDERS
Steve Mensing

Wade Walker's kid brother, Duane, was locked up in the Silver City jail facing a rope at dawn. Wade was a ruthless outlaw, but he was smart, and he had vowed to have his brother out of jail before morning!

DESERT OF THE DAMNED
Nelson Nye

The law was after him for the murder of a marshal — a murder he didn't commit. Breen was after him for revenge — and Breen wouldn't stop at anything . . . blackmail, a frameup . . . or murder.

DAY OF THE COMANCHEROS
Steven C. Lawrence

Their very name struck terror into men's hearts — the Comancheros, a savage army of cutthroats who swept across Texas, leaving behind a bloodstained trail of robbery and murder.

SUNDANCE: SILENT ENEMY
John Benteen

A lone crazed Cheyenne was on a personal war path. They needed to pit one man against one crazed Indian. That man was Sundance.

LASSITER
Jack Slade

Lassiter wasn't the kind of man to listen to reason. Cross him once and he'll hold a grudge for years to come — if he let you live that long.

LAST STAGE TO GOMORRAH
Barry Cord

Jeff Carter, tough ex-riverboat gambler, now had himself a horse ranch that kept him free from gunfights and card games. Until Sturvesant of Wells Fargo showed up.

McALLISTER
ON THE
COMANCHE CROSSING
Matt Chisholm

The Comanche, McAllister owes them a life — and the trail is soaked with the blood of the men who had tried to outrun them before.

QUICK-TRIGGER COUNTRY
Clem Colt

Turkey Red hooked up with Curly Bill Graham's outlaw crew. But wholesale murder was out of Turk's line, so when range war flared he bucked the whole border gang alone . . .

CAMPAIGNING
Jim Miller

Ambushed on the Santa Fe trail, Sean Callahan is saved by two Indian strangers. But there'll be more lead and arrows flying before the band join Kit Carson against the Comanches.

GUNSLINGER'S RANGE
Jackson Cole

Three escaped convicts are out for revenge. They won't rest until they put a bullet through the head of the dirty snake who locked them behind bars.

RUSTLER'S TRAIL
Lee Floren

Jim Carlin knew he would have to stand up and fight because he had staked his claim right in the middle of Big Ike Outland's best grass.

THE TRUTH ABOUT SNAKE RIDGE
Marshall Grover

The troubleshooters came to San Cristobal to help the needy. For Larry and Stretch the turmoil began with a brawl and then an ambush.

WOLF DOG RANGE
Lee Floren

Will Ardery would stop at nothing, unless something stopped him first — like a bullet from Pete Manly's gun.

DEVIL'S DINERO
Marshall Grover

Plagued by remorse, a rich old reprobate hired the Texas Troubleshooters to deliver a fortune in greenbacks to each of his victims.

GUNS OF FURY
Ernest Haycox

Dane Starr, alias Dan Smith, wanted to close the door on his past and hang up his guns, but people wouldn't let him.